No matter how settled she feels in her new life, Alisa fears the past will resurface.

The bell chimed above the door. Alisa turned, expecting to see Titus standing there.

"Well, looky here, Amos. We don't got to look no farther."

"I told you two weeks ago we shoulda come here in the first place, but you had to take us hither and yon."

"Shut up, Amos."

"What are you talking about?" Mrs. White asked.

"The girl. She's wanted in San Francisco, and we come to fetch her back."

"You the law?" Mrs. White eyed the two.

Hysterical laughter bubbled from Alisa's lips. "The law? These are the two men who robbed the stagecoach the day I arrived."

"Then they can forget taking you anywhere."

Bart took a menacing step forward. "Now you just be a nice old lady and don't cause a fuss, and no one'll get hurt. One way or another, we're taking her with us."

TRACEY V. BATEMAN lives with her husband and four children in southwest Missouri. She believes in a strong church family relationship and sings on the worship team. Serving as vice president of American Christian Romance Writers gives Tracey the opportunity to help new writers work toward their writing goals.

Books by Tracey V. Bateman

HEARTSONG PRESENTS

Don't miss out on any of our super romances. Write to us at the following address for information on our newest releases and club information.

Heartsong Presents Readers' Service
PO Box 719
Uhrichsville, OH 44683

Or visit www.heartsongpresents.com

Second Chance

Tracey V. Bateman

Heartsong Presents

To Nancy Toback. I love you.

Special thanks to Chris Lynxwiler and Pamela Griffin for whirlwind critiques and faithful friendship.

A note from the Author:
I love to hear from my readers! You may correspond with me by writing:

Tracey V. Bateman
Author Relations
PO Box 719
Uhrichsville, OH 44683

ISBN 1-59310-182-1

SECOND CHANCE

Our mission is to publish and distribute inspirational products offering exceptional value and biblical encouragement to the masses.

All scripture quotations are taken from the King James Version of the Bible.

All of the characters and events in this book are fictitious. Any resemblance to actual persons, living or dead, or to actual events is purely coincidental.

PRINTED IN THE U.S.A.

Or check out our Web site at www.heartsongpresents.com

prologue

San Francisco, 1871

"I'm leaving the house and the money to Alisa."

Standing with her back pressed against the wall outside the library, Alisa touched her fingers to her throat. Alarm inched its way up her spine. What could Mrs. Worthington possibly be thinking by telling her son such an outlandish tale? She inched around so that she could peer through the small crack where the door wasn't quite shut all the way. The dear woman sat regally in a black leather chair behind her husband's desk, her fingers laced together as she conversed with her son.

"Surely, you're joking, Mother. Leave our money to a foundling?"

"A foundling who should never have been lost in the first place."

"Please, Mother." The sound of Mr. Worthington's long-suffering voice rankled Alisa. He should show his mother more respect, in her opinion. "Must you always throw that little indiscretion in my face?"

"That darling child is much more than an indiscretion in my eyes. I'm so thankful to God that we found her before she left the orphanage. My only heartbreak is that it took so many years to locate her. Now that I have all the legalities taken care of so that you can't prevent it from happening,

5

I am ready to tell her of her true heritage and welcome her into the family."

Alisa shifted her gaze so that she could see Mr. Worthington. He stood by the stone fireplace, one of his elbows resting on the mantel. He leaned his forehead into the palm of one hand and gave a short laugh. "And what of me, Mother? You raised me accustomed to a certain standard of living. How do you expect me to fend for myself? Have you only love for the girl? None for your son?"

"Of course I love you, my boy. And it's true, you were much too spoiled for your own good. As for your well-being, you still own seventy-five percent of the shipping business. Alisa will own the other twenty-five percent so that she may live in comfort the rest of her life."

Frustrated by her obscured view, Alisa dared to push at the door, widening the crack so that she could see both Mrs. Worthington and her son. What was the elderly woman saying? Had her mind suddenly become unhinged? In the three months since she'd come to work for Mrs. Worthington as her companion, she'd noticed peculiarities in the way she was treated more highly than most servants. But what possessed the woman to even consider leaving her a penny, let alone part of a company? And this beautiful home?

Mr. Worthington stalked across the room, his boots clacking on the hardwood floor. He leaned across the desk. "I'll have you declared incompetent, Mother. I don't want to, but I will if you force me to."

"I thought you might try that one." She sighed. "Why do greedy children always think it's so easy to declare an old woman feebleminded? Son, I've already made the changes to the will in the presence of five witnesses, just to be safe."

Robert's fist came down hard on the sleek mahogany desktop. "I'll contest the will. I'll make the courts believe the girl tricked you into leaving her an inheritance. My inheritance."

Mrs. Worthington pushed back from the desk. Leaning heavily on her cane, she lifted herself from her chair. She limped to Robert's side. "There is nothing you can do. If you contest, the entire city will see you as a cad and a fool."

"If reputation is so important to you, why are you leaving everything to that. . ."

Alisa gasped at the vile word he used to describe her. While growing up in the orphanage, all of her dreams included a beautiful mother and a handsome father. They were dressed in white each time they returned to get her. What a joyous reunion it was every night while she slept. Her mother's soft kisses, her father's strong arms. Never once had Alisa considered that she might be illegitimate. Her wonderful dream had turned to a nightmare with one filthy word.

Mrs. Worthington struck with her veiny, bony hand and left a print on his cheek as a loud slap resounded through the library. "You've no right to call her that. No right at all. I've made arrangements to legitimize her. She will be given the family name."

Alisa *Worthington*.

"I'll not stand for it!"

"I'm afraid you've no choice in the matter. You should have done right by her years ago; then I wouldn't be forced to bring this embarrassment on you now. She will be introduced into society as my granddaughter during the Christmas ball."

"Never!"

Still trying to grasp the enormity of what Mrs. Worthington had just spoken, Alisa watched in horror as Mr. Worthington took the elderly lady by the shoulders and shook her hard.

"Stop it!" Alisa leaped from her hiding place. "Turn her loose!"

Startled by the sudden interruption, he released her. Mrs. Worthington stumbled back, grabbing the edge of the desk to steady herself.

"How dare you eavesdrop on a private conversation!" the man spouted.

Ignoring him, Alisa gently took Mrs. Worthington by the shoulders. "Are you all right, ma'am?"

A smile creased the lined face. She reached up and patted Alisa's cheek. "You may call me Grandmother, my dear."

Tears sprang to Alisa's eyes. "You don't know what you're saying, Mrs. Worthington. Let's get you settled back into your chair."

"Wait." She pressed her fist to her heart and grimaced.

"Are you all right?"

"I will be. Listen to me now, darling girl. I've searched for you since you were a baby."

"Me, ma'am?"

"Yes. Your mother was the daughter of a laundress who worked out by the docks. She caught Robert's eye and. . .well, you can imagine how you came to be."

"But I don't understand how you could possibly know I am the child of that union."

"But I can and do. When your mother's time came, she bravely came to our home for help. You were born soon after she arrived. I was privileged to assist in your birth. Afterward, I held you and rocked you while she slept. You were ever so precious."

"Mother, stop filling her head with this nonsense."

Alisa stared at the man standing next to her. All of her dreams of some day having a father died, and without warning, tears sprang to her eyes. Mr. Worthington's face reddened, and his gaze faltered.

Mrs. Worthington touched Alisa's cheek to regain her attention. The old, tired eyes held a look of such love that Alisa knew the precious lady believed every word she spoke. "I wrapped you in your father's baby blanket and placed you next to your mother. Then I retired to my own room. When I awoke to your mother's screaming, I knew Robert had taken you away. He returned later that evening and told me he had given you to a childless couple and that you were sailing for England that very night. I was heartbroken but powerless. The next morning your mother was gone, and she never returned."

"Then. . .how did you. . . ?"

"A maid from the household had disappeared the same night you were born. In those days, we took in all sorts. About a year ago, she came back looking for work. I couldn't hire her, for she stank of spirits, and she told me, in spite, about taking my grandchild to an orphanage. I hired a detective agency, and they combed the city. A few months later, we found you."

Alisa's thoughts went to the worn blanket she kept tucked away for safekeeping. "And when you described the blanket, Mrs. Perryman knew I was the one?"

"Yes. That is exactly how we came to find you."

"I can't believe it. I have a grandmother?"

"No, you do not."

Alisa shrank from the man she now knew to be her father, as he towered over her.

"I refuse to allow you to take advantage of an old woman's delusions."

A gasp escaped Alisa's throat. "But I would never take advantage."

"Of course she wouldn't. And I'm far from delusional. Leave the girl alone, Robert. She most certainly does have a grandmother." Mrs. Worthington moaned softly and pressed her hand more tightly against her chest. "I. . .believe I. . . must. . .sit."

Filled with alarm, Alisa tried to tighten her hold just as Mrs. Worthington stiffened, clutched her chest, and slipped from Alisa's grasp. Time seemed to slow as she watched in horror. The elderly woman crashed to the ground, her head hitting against the edge of the desk as she fell.

"I am sorry to interrupt but. . .Madam!" Marietta, Mrs. Worthington's housekeeper of forty years, stood just inside the room. Her silver tray clattered to the floor as she rushed to her mistress's side.

"Mrs. Worthington!" Alisa dropped to her knees. Blood ran from a gash on the elderly lady's forehead.

"What have you done, girl?" Mr. Worthington grabbed her roughly and flung her away. He knelt beside his mother.

"Is she going to be all right?" Tears streamed down Marietta's face.

"Mother? Mother, please open your eyes and talk to me."

The elderly woman lay motionless.

Alicia caught her breath as Mr. Worthington's venomous gaze swept over her. "Marietta, go fetch the doctor and the police. My mother has been murdered."

one

"Throw down that six-shooter, mister. Then empty out yer pockets."

Titus Chance glared at the two men—not men really, but cowards, who had to cover their faces with bandanas. Cowards who couldn't win in a fair fight, so they had to sneak up on him while he dozed beside his campfire. But lily livers or no, they had two guns to his one, and he wasn't riled enough to be a fool.

He tossed his Colt to the dusty earth. Reaching slowly into his pockets, he pulled out twenty dollars and a gold money clip and pitched those on the ground as well.

The burly leader fingered the bills. "That all you got?"

" 'Fraid so." At least that was all he had in his pocket.

Piercing eyes bored through him. Titus stared back, careful to keep his expression as innocent as a newborn babe's.

Titus balled his fists as he watched the thief shift his gaze. "That's a fine little horse you got there. I'd say it'll make up for you not having enough cash to make this worth my time. Amos, get the horse."

The other rider jerked his head toward the leader. "But we can't jest leave a feller out here in the middle of nowhere without a horse, Bart. Besides, stealing a little money is one thing. I ain't no horse thief. They can hang a man for that."

"They can hang ya for stealing money, too. Now do as I say." He expelled a frustrated grunt. "And what have I told you

11

about calling me by my name while we're robbing someone?"

"Well, I don't like it," Amos said, but he dismounted his horse and headed toward Titus, his pistol pulled and threatening. "Back off easy-like, mister, and don't make me use this."

If the situation hadn't been so grave, Titus might have laughed at the bumbling crooks. But bumbling or no, they still had the guns, and he didn't. And if he had a prayer of a chance of getting out of this situation alive, he had to be smarter than they were. Which actually didn't seem all that far of a stretch.

He backed away from the mare he'd raised since birth. He'd named her Raven for her beautiful black coat. Swallowing hard, he kept a cautious gaze on the men as Amos took Raven's reins. The horse reared only for a second, long enough for Titus to dive for his Colt. He landed with a painful thud on his stomach and slid until he reached his gun. But he wasn't fast enough. One of the ruffians kicked dirt into his eyes, blinding him. "Yer lucky we don't kill ya fer that stunt. Mount up, Amos, and let's git."

When they'd gone, Titus crawled sightless until he reached the lake. After he'd washed the dirt from his eyes, he sat back and slapped his thigh in frustration.

Now what was he supposed to do? He'd left home a few days ago—directly after Priscilla White had refused his proposal. It had been at his sister-in-law's insistence that he'd left for a few days. "One grouch around here is plenty," Miriam had said, waving a wooden spoon in his face. She jerked her head at Daniel. "And my other brother-in-law already has that position filled." She said it with a twinkle in her eyes to remove the sting, but Titus knew she was right. He'd been moping long enough.

Daniel—who really was a grouch like Miriam said—had

gotten up and stomped out of the house, while her husband, Gideon, laughed uproariously. Titus hadn't necessarily thought it funny, but Gideon was a new husband and thought anything his new bride said or did to be brilliant and inspired.

So Titus had taken a few days to pull himself together, mourn the loss of the woman he'd convinced himself he was destined to wed, and generally shake off his foul mood. San Francisco wasn't too far away. Close enough that he could make it there in a few hours if he started walking now. He could catch the stage out to Reliable. From there he could rent a horse to ride to the ranch.

He walked back to the campfire and sat down, knowing he'd have to wait until dawn to head back to the city. Feeling like a fool for letting himself get robbed in the first place, he stretched out on the ground and spent the night listening for noises that might indicate the thieves had returned.

By first light, he was up and headed back to San Francisco, relieved beyond measure that the thieves hadn't been smart enough to tell him to empty his boot, the place where he'd hidden most of his money.

❧

Alisa eyed the mother and son sitting next to her on the seat.

"Davy, please, eat your bread for Mama." The woman's soft, pleading tone filled the inside of the stagecoach, annoying Alisa more than the boy's constant kicking against the seat.

After two days without a decent meal, she would have gladly snatched at the bread and gobbled it down in front of the ungrateful child. He kicked the bottom of the seat with the backs of his heels over and over and over until Alisa was tempted to place her hand gently on his swinging legs and order him to stop.

He held his bread in one hand and rubbed a chubby little fist over his eye.

"Oh, is Mama's boy sleepy?"

"No!" he yelled and kicked his feet higher and harder.

"Of course you are. That's why you're acting so unruly."

Alisa ventured a glance at the dark-haired cowboy sitting across from her. His head rested on the back of the seat; and his hat covered his face. His shoulders rose and fell with an almost unbelievable rhythm. How on earth could he sleep through all the racket that annoying boy was making?

"I'm truly sorry," the young mother intoned.

Alisa tore her gaze away from the handsome man. The mother's lips curved into a weary smile. "He's really a lovely child," she tried to explain. "We've been traveling several days, and he's so very tired."

"I'm not tired!" the boy insisted at a feverish pitch.

"Mama believes you."

Despite a deplorable lack of disciplinary action on the young mother's part, Alisa had to admire the woman's calm. Her own patience had worn thin an hour ago. The young mother looked at the boy and patted her thighs. "How would you like to sit on my lap?"

She winked at Alisa, and Alisa couldn't resist the dimples flashing in the young woman's cheeks. She smiled back.

Davy set his bread down on the bench and climbed into his mother's lap. Before long, both were dozing.

Alisa's empty stomach rumbled in protest as she stared at the half-eaten bread still sitting where it had been flung. It was all she could do not to snatch it up and wolf it down. After two full nights and a day of wandering around San Francisco in case she was being followed, and then half a day so far on the stage without food, her head felt light, and she almost wept from hunger. She'd been holding her reticule, about to visit the orphanage, when she'd heard Mrs. Worthington's voice from the hallway outside of the library door. The only money her reticule held was the donation she'd intended to leave with Mrs. Perryman, the woman who ran the orphanage. The amount was just enough for her stage ticket.

The chubby five-year-old boy was now fast asleep in his mother's arms, and the bread just sat there like a shiny pot of gold at the end of the rainbow.

She slid her hand along the bench then snatched it back as the child shifted, causing his mother's head to snap up and her eyes to fly open. "Are we there yet?"

"No. You've only just dozed off," Alisa said, guilt searing her heart. *Thank you, dear Lord, for not allowing my hunger to cause me to sin.* She shuddered to think how close she'd come to stealing a little boy's bread.

The woman's eyes had drifted shut once more. Alisa ogled the bread for one last second, then willfully turned her entire body away. As she shifted, she came face-to-face with the cowboy. Only this time he wasn't sleeping. He stared at her with oh-so-blue eyes. Eyes filled with. . .pity.

Horror sank into the pit of her stomach. He must have seen her almost take the bread. Heat flashed to her cheeks. She covered her face with her hands, too ashamed to look him in the eye. He tapped her forearm. Shaking her head, she flexed her muscles to press her face harder into her palms. Oh, she had never been more humiliated.

"Look at me," he whispered.

Reluctantly, she glanced up, tears already pooling in her eyes.

He gave her a gentle smile. "Take this."

She looked down at the beef jerky in his hands. "I. . .I couldn't." She *couldn't* look away. Before she could stop herself, she licked her lips like a wolf eyeing a tasty rabbit just before it pounced.

"Take it, miss," he urged. "I have more."

Unable to resist a second longer, she took it. "Th. . .thank you," she whispered.

He nodded. Thankfully, he leaned back and covered his face once more with his hat while she gnawed the dried meat, savoring it as though it were a juicy chicken leg.

≈

San Francisco

"I am sorry, Mr. Worthington, but there is nothing we can do. Your mother left no detail to chance. I assure you, her will is binding."

"I can fight it in court. Then we'll see how binding it is."

Frank Chadwick, Mrs. Worthington's long-standing attorney, glowered, and Robert could tell he was fighting to stay calm. "I seriously doubt any judge will be inclined to award you the estate, particularly after you tried to frame the girl for your mother's murder."

"How was I to know Mother's heart failed?"

"To say the girl pushed her and demanded money was a deliberate ploy so that you could contest the will."

Yes, and it would have worked if the housekeeper hadn't seen Mother slip out of Alisa's grasp and the girl try desperately to save her.

"So I'm left with only the company?"

"Seventy-five *percent* of the company." Mr. Chadwick leaned forward. "The girl, should she be found, will be awarded the house and all of its contents, twenty-five percent of the shipping company, and the money in all the accounts, with the exception of two thousand dollars. Your mother thought you might need it to tide you over for a few weeks. By then you should be receiving revenue from the shipping company."

Robert leaned back against the brown leather chair. Mr. Chadwick smiled—most smugly—his fingers steepled in front of him.

Two thousand dollars. That wouldn't pay much of anything. Robert knew Mother had at least three million dollars sitting in those accounts. Nausea nearly overwhelmed his stomach at the thought of all that money going to the girl. It would take him thirty years to make back that kind of cash with the income from seventy-five percent of the business. What right did she have to it? He felt no responsibility, no affection for the girl who carried his blood in her veins. Truth be told, there could easily be a dozen more just like her between here and England. He didn't know, nor did he care.

"And if the girl isn't found?" He could make sure she wasn't if necessary.

Chadwick narrowed his gaze. "The money will stay in an account for ten years, at the end of which time it will be given to charities."

"Charity?"

"Your mother was quite firm about the matter."

"What are my choices if I am to prevent this young woman from stealing my inheritance?"

The lawyer's lip curled in poorly disguised disgust, but Robert didn't care. Let *him* lose three million dollars and his childhood home and see how he'd behave.

"Well?" Robert demanded.

"You can always find her, speak with her, and if she is willing to sign over her rights to the house and the money, then I suppose they would go to you."

Hope flickered anew in Robert. Then that's what he'd do. Put out ads all over the state. Post a reward. One thousand dollars. No, he only had two. On the other hand, if the girl was found, he'd have more than enough to pay a reward. Five hundred.

He stood and extended his hand. "Thank you, Frank. You've been most helpful."

two

A cramp in his leg pulled Titus rudely from sleep. He sat up straight, rubbing at the knot in his thigh, and took his hat from his face. After being awake throughout the night and walking all the way to San Francisco, he was worn clear through. But at least he wasn't hungry. Not like the girl sitting across from him. He hadn't offered her another strip of meat. No sense adding to her humiliation. Poor thing. His heart clenched at the memory of her staring at the kid's bread.

She slept, her head resting against the wall. The open window sent a breeze through the stagecoach and lifted wayward strands of auburn hair from her forehead. Titus swallowed hard at the sight. Her long lashes framed beautiful, enormous eyes and brushed the tops of her cheeks as she slept. His brow furrowed at the sight of the dark circles. She'd undoubtedly lost as much sleep as he had. But why? What possessed a woman to spend her last dime on a stage ticket? She had no luggage that he'd seen. Only a small reticule that she clutched tightly even in sleep. Everything about her indicated a woman on the run.

The stage hit a hole and jostled. A shuddering breath lifted her shoulders. She opened her eyes, sitting up as she did so. She looked straight at him, and her eyes widened.

Caught staring, Titus sent her a sheepish grin. He thought he detected a twitch of her lips before she averted her gaze to the window.

"How long until we reach Reliable?" The low, sleep-induced huskiness of her voice was alluring, he had to admit. A bit of guilt niggled at him for thinking it; after all, he'd been jilted less than a week ago.

He glanced out the window, barely remembering to answer her question. "I'd say no more than three or four hours." He tipped his hat. "I'm Titus Chance. My family owns a ranch not far from Reliable. You got family there?"

She shook her head. "N. . .no."

"Mail-order bride?"

Her face reddened. "No."

"So, no folks, no husband waiting?" For some reason his heart lightened at the last bit of information. Still he hated the thought of her being alone. "Do you have friends? Or at the very least a position of employment waiting?" His throat dried out in a split second as he mentally ran through a list of possible employers.

"I have no one and no job."

"Well, if you don't mind my saying so, Reliable might not be the best choice of a town for a pretty young woman all alone." He smiled to take the sting out of his words, but what happened next filled him with horror.

Her lovely brown eyes filled with tears.

He swallowed hard and fumbled in his pocket for a hand-kerchief. "Please don't cry, miss." He should be shot. Why did he always have to blurt out the truth?

"Oh, it's not your fault. I cry far too easily. I. . .I don't know what I'll do if there's nothing for me in Reliable." She eyed him. "I mean respectable employment."

It was Titus's turn to blush. He couldn't think of anything that she could do. In a young town the size of Reliable, there weren't many positions available for a decent woman. But he planned to see what he could do. He knew enough people that surely someone would take her in.

"You didn't tell me your name."

"Alisa."

He smiled. "Alisa what?"

She hesitated then squared her shoulders. "My name is Alisa Worthington." She said the words like an announcement.

"Nice to meet you Miss Worthington. Would you care to have dinner with me?"

"Dinner?"

He grinned and reached into his bag. "It's not much," he said giving her a strip of the jerky.

"You've been too kind already." She eyed the meat hungrily.

"Nonsense." He offered it again. This time she took it.

"Thank you."

"I hate to eat alone."

A pretty smile lifted the corners of her lips.

Titus almost choked on his bite of jerky. He hadn't realized how badly he'd wanted to see her smile. The sight of it brightened the entire inside of the stagecoach as far as he was concerned.

A giggle from the other side of the stagecoach captured his attention. He turned to find the woman next to Miss Worthington grinning at him. She sent him a broad wink. His ears burned to have been so transparent.

To his profound relief, she didn't dwell on the situation. Instead, she stretched and moved the still-sleeping little boy onto the seat. He mumbled and shifted and finally ended up with his head resting against Miss Worthington's shoulder.

"Do you mind?" the child's mother asked. "I'm worn clean

through. He sure isn't the teensy baby he once was." With a weary huff, she glanced out the window, then back to Titus. "How far do we have to go?" she asked.

"Only a couple more hours."

"Oh, I will be so glad to be done with trains and stage-coaches. I never plan to travel again."

"Do you have family in town?" Titus asked, more to be polite than from a desire to know.

"My brother, Aaron Bladdel. Do you know him?"

"The blacksmith? Sure. I didn't realize he had a sister."

She laughed, and her twinkling blue eyes set in a chubby-cheeked face make him feel more at ease. "I suppose I should be insulted that he hasn't mentioned me."

"We talk more business than anything."

"Then I suppose I'll forgive him."

Titus returned her smile. "Will your husband be join-ing you?"

Her expression crashed. "No. I'm afraid my Henry passed on a few weeks ago. That's why Davy and I are here."

Miss Worthington reached around Davy and patted her hand. "I am so sorry, Mrs. . . ." She glanced at Titus for sup-port, but he hadn't caught the woman's name either.

"Ah, well." The woman pulled a lace handkerchief from her bag and dabbed at her eyes. "There's no point in crying. It only upsets Davy. And my name is Mrs. Greene. Violet Greene." She smiled. "Henry always laughed at my name. Two colors."

Titus had to admire her spirit. He didn't want to bring it up, but he doubted seriously she'd be long without a husband. Not in a town where the men outnumbered the women about twenty to one.

Of course that applied to Miss Worthington, too. Now that

thought stuck in his craw, and it was mighty uncomfortable!

❧

Alisa's arm was growing numb by the time Davy woke up and glared at her as though she'd been the one to pull him from the safety and warmth of his mother's lap.

"I'm thirsty, Mommy."

"I know, sweetheart. We will be in Reliable very soon, and I will get you a drink."

"I'm thirsty now!"

"I'm sorry, but the water is all gone. You drank it to wash down your lunch, remember? I told you that was all."

Mr. Chance slipped his hand into his saddlebag and produced a canteen.

"Oh, we couldn't," Mrs. Greene insisted.

"I have plenty." He winked at Davy. "Can't have the boy thirsty. Take some for yourself as well and pass it to Miss Worthington."

The little boy gulped noisily, then heaved a sigh and began swinging his legs, thumping the bottom of the seat as he had earlier.

Alisa pressed her fingertips to her temple, trying to ward off the mounting ache.

"Hey, little fella," Mr. Chance said, smiling at Davy. "How about not kicking that seat?"

The child scowled and turned his face to his mother's arm, but he continued to thump the seat. "I'm so sorry," Mrs. Greene said. "It's difficult for him to keep still."

"It's all right," Alisa said. She'd never seen such a poorly behaved child. Growing up in an orphanage had taught her obedience. Though her upbringing had not been harsh, it was most definitely strict.

Trying to ignore the pain in her head, now throbbing in time to the kicks of Davy's boots against the seat, she glanced out the window. In the distance, she saw riders coming. She turned to alert Mr. Chance, but his gaze, too, was focused toward the horizon. A muscle jerked in his jaw.

A sense of unease crept through Alisa as she felt his tension. His hand went to his gun belt. It was empty. Frustration crossed his features.

"Is everything all right, Mr. Chance?"

"The men coming are not the welcoming party from Reliable," he said in a matter-of-fact tone.

"Oh, Reliable has a welcoming party?" Mrs. Greene asked.

Alisa fought the urge to roll her eyes. "I believe Mr. Chance is saying the men coming are up to no good."

Mr. Chance nodded gravely. "You're right, Miss Worthington. I'm afraid those are the same men who robbed me last night. They took my gun and my horse and all the money I had in my pocket."

Mrs. Greene let out a little shriek and grabbed Davy close. "Oh my."

"Mr. Wayne?" the cowboy called to the stage master.

"I see 'em," came the rough reply. "Yaw!" he yelled to the horses, and the stage sped up.

But even Alisa could see there would be no outrunning two men on horseback. "What should we do, Mr. Chance?"

"Unless you have a pistol hidden in that bag of yours, I suggest we pray." He hesitated; then he gave what Alisa was sure was supposed to have been a reassuring smile. However, it fell short of doing any such thing. "If they were out to truly do any harm, I'm sure they would have done more than kick dirt in my face and steal my horse."

"They kicked dirt in your face?" Mrs. Greene asked. "How awful."

"Not so awful as a bullet," Mr. Chance retorted absently. Alisa had to agree.

Gunfire sounded, and the stage master pulled the stage to a stop. The two bandits held pistols upright. A series of shots fired into the air. They ordered the wagon master to throw down his weapons and climb down. Then a gravelly voice called out, "All right. Get out. All of you."

Alisa looked to Mr. Chance for instruction. He nodded and opened the stage door. "I'll go first." He climbed down, then turned and offered his assistance to Alisa. Next he lifted Davy from the stage then helped Mrs. Greene.

"That all of ya?" one of the bandits asked.

"Yes." Mr. Chance stood, fists clenched.

Recognition flashed in the bandit's dark eyes. "Well, Amos, looky here. This feller jest ain't very lucky."

The other man chuckled. "Didn't we make yer acquaintance last night? Yep, that's one nice Colt ya give us." He patted the sleek neck of the horse he had just dismounted. "And this girl here is one beaut of a horse."

The cowboy grinned back, and Alisa frowned. What was he up to?

"I suppose this surely isn't my lucky day, but I have to tell you. . .it's not yours either."

"How do ya figure that?"

"Well, considering you forced me to empty my pockets last night, you won't find anything of value on me. And this young lady didn't even have. . ."

Alisa drew in a breath. Would he humiliate her just to prove the point that if she couldn't feed herself, she probably couldn't give them anything of value?

"A trunk," he said, completing his observation. Despite her precarious situation, Alisa's heart swelled with gratitude. Mr. Chance personified all the heroes in her dime books—the stories she hadn't been allowed to read when she lived at the orphanage. But since becoming Mrs. Worthington's companion, Alisa read everything she could get her hands on, dime books included.

He continued goading the thieves. "The other young lady is widowed and traveling to Reliable to live with her brother because she can't raise her son alone."

"I thought you said there was a senator on this here stage, Bart."

"Can I help it if that drunk varmint back at the Lucky Hand Saloon lied to me?" The man eyed his partner. "And what have I told you about calling me by my name?"

"Sorry, Bar. . .Joe."

Alisa stifled a giggle behind her hand.

"All right, gimme whatever ya got," the one called Bart said. He held out his hat as though passing around the offering plate.

Scurrying to obey, Mrs. Greene opened her satchel and tossed a wad of money into the hat. Alisa's eyes widened, and she stared at the woman. "M. . .my husband was well off. I never said I came west because I was poor. Although, after today, that is certainly going to be my circumstance."

"Yee haw!"

Alisa jumped as Amos grabbed the hat away from Bart. He stopped in front of Mr. Chance. "Not our lucky day, huh? Well then what do you call this?"

The cowboy glared but kept his mouth shut. Alisa couldn't

help but be relieved. A man capable of robbery might also be capable of violence if provoked.

The man came to her. "Well? Whadda you got, girlie? Or am I gonna have to search ya?"

Mr. Chance stepped forward. "Keep your filthy hands off her. She has nothing."

"I'll see that fer myself."

Alisa showed him her reticule. "A. . .all that I have is a handkerchief."

"That all? Well, maybe I'll take a kiss instead."

Shrinking back in alarm, Alisa felt the blood rushing to her head. She grabbed Mr. Chance's arm to keep from losing her balance.

"I thought I told you to leave her alone!" He reached out to grab Amos just as Bart's gun fired.

Alisa stared in horror as Mr. Chance slipped from her grasp. He landed with a thud on the ground, blood spilling from a wound in his temple.

three

Titus slowly came to, pain slicing his temple. Pebbles ground into his back—evidence he was lying on hard ground. His head, however, was pillowed in something soft and elevated off the ground. Gentle fingers pushed back the hair from his forehead and pressed a wet cloth to his temple. He opened his eyes.

Miss Worthington?

"Oh, thank You, Lord," she breathed. "He's coming around."

Was he dreaming? Or was Miss Worthington even prettier from this angle? He started to sit up, but a wave of dizziness sent him back to. . .Miss Worthington's lap? If this was a dream, may he never wake up!

"How are you feeling, Mr. Chance?"

He offered her a wobbly smile. "Like I've been shot. What happened? I'm obviously not dead. Unless, of course, you're an angel."

A beguiling blush darkened her rosy cheeks. "I'm afraid you're still mortal, Mr. Chance. And I most certainly am as well."

A shadow blocked the glow of the retreating sun. The stage master stood over him. "Well, if that bullet had been a little more to the left, he wouldn't be with us. As it is, he's going to have a monster of a headache for a few days from that nick." His gravelly voice held not a trace of sympathy. Like a grizzled westerner, he stated the simple facts. "Them varmints took off like a couple of scared jackrabbits after you pitched to the ground. Lucky for you they couldn't hit the broad side of a barn with a sawed-off shotgun."

It had nothing to do with luck, he thought, at the same time Miss Worthington said, "Luck had nothing to do with it, Mr. Wayne. God surely had his hand on Mr. Chance."

Hmmm. He gazed into her suspiciously moist eyes and smiled. She smiled back. "Are you able to get up now?"

He'd rather just stay there forever, close his eyes, and relieve the pain in his head, but he couldn't take advantage of her generous spirit and soft lap any longer. He sat up again, this time with her assistance. The world spun for a moment. Miss Worthington handed him the wet handkerchief she'd been holding against his head.

"Thank you."

His gaze locked onto hers, and he felt time stand still. How could he have ever believed himself in love with a woman like Prissy White? He couldn't even remember what she looked like, except for the ridiculous false blond curls she'd recently taken to wearing. Funny, two weeks ago, he'd found them attractive. But that was before he'd met Miss Worthington. And right now she seemed to be having as much trouble looking away as he was having.

Mr. Wayne stepped forward and offered his hand. "Well, let's get you back into the stage. I got a schedule to keep."

Titus groaned as pain stabbed his head. Movement wasn't necessarily a good thing, but he gritted his teeth and closed his eyes as the stage master hefted him to his feet. Miss Worthington stood on one side of him. He swayed as the world spun. The gentle pressure of her palm heated his back. "It's all right, Mr. Chance. I won't let you fall."

Her gentle, sincere voice made him smile, despite the pain. If he'd been feeling better, he'd have asked her who would hold her up if he started to fall. Instead, he accepted her assistance to the stage. She climbed in ahead of him and then offered her hands while Mr. Wayne helped him from behind. When he was finally settled into the seat, his head throbbed. All he wanted was to lie down and sleep. Since the cramped interior and narrow seat prevented him from doing so, he stretched out sideways as much as possible and slumped against the window.

Mrs. Greene gasped softly. As she had been earlier, she sat next to Miss Worthington, clutching Davy tightly in her grasp. "Oh, I am so relieved that you are all right, Mr. Chance. I just knew that bullet went through your head. I had to bring Davy inside so he didn't have to see all the blood. He's very sensitive. I feared for his peace of mind."

"The bullet only grazed Mr. Chance," Alisa broke in, much to Titus's relief. He didn't feel like talking, as his stomach was beginning to rebel against the jostle of the stagecoach, not to mention the vivid image of his blood spilling on the ground. *Thank You, Lord for steering that bullet away from my skull.*

Regrettably, Mrs. Greene didn't take the hint. "Oh, that is fortunate for you. I once knew a man who—"

Titus closed his eyes against the pain.

"Perhaps we should let Mr. Chance rest." Titus heard the sweetness of Miss Worthington's voice just as he drifted to sleep.

He awoke to the same sweet voice. "Wake up, Mr. Chance. We've arrived in Reliable."

His head throbbed, but he smiled. He could get used to waking up to that sound every day. When he opened his eyes, she was leaning forward, concern plainly written in her expression. As he met her gaze, relief replaced concern. His first attempt to sit up straight failed as a bolt of pain sent him back to the seat with a moan.

"Sit up slowly," Miss Worthington admonished.

It felt good to have a woman fuss over him. And even more so when she placed her hand on his side and gently helped him to an upright position. Gideon's assessment of things had sure been right. There was nothing like a woman's touch. Of course, Gideon was a happily married man. Not just any woman's touch would do. Take Prissy for instance. Her hand tucked inside the crook of his arm had never sent shocks of warmth down his spine. Now, Miss Worthington was a different matter altogether. He could barely remember where he was when he was so close to this woman. And he was almost certain the near-amnesia was due to the sweetness of her touch and not his wound.

Clarity slowly replaced his confusion, and he glanced through the window as the stage rolled to a halt in front of an eating establishment.

"I have never been so happy to see a dusty old town in my life!" Mrs. Greene said, and Titus had to agree with her. The stage master opened the door.

"Everyone out. We're behind as it is. Other folks are waitin'. There's dinner waitin' inside iffen you can pay for it."

"My, oh my, I am famished." Mrs. Greene climbed out of the coach and reached around for Davy. "Are you hungry, darling? It's a good thing Mommy had some money hidden away from those bad, bad men." She turned to Titus and Miss Worthington. "It was so nice meeting you both. I am sure in a town this size, we will meet again. Say good-bye, Davy."

"Bye." The farewell was hardly discernable as the chubby little boy's attention was averted to the source of food. He yanked on his mother's hand. "Come on, Mama."

With a final dimpled smile, Mrs. Greene stepped inside the diner. The dinnertime smells wafting from the building tempted Titus's stomach. He could only guess how the aroma of roasted meat and freshly baked bread was affecting Miss Worthington.

She looked around, her lip clasped between her teeth, brow furrowed. Titus's heart went out to her. What was she going to do? Where on earth would she sleep? The sun had set two hours earlier. Even if she were to find work, it certainly wouldn't be tonight. At that moment, chivalry was born in Titus's heart. There was no getting around it. He would help her. His heart had already made the choice for him, and there was nothing to do but follow along.

He would need help getting home; there was no question about that. If it was daylight, the solution would be obvious. Hire a team and buggy from the livery and appeal to her sense of pity. But no decent woman would agree to spending so much as an hour in the dark traveling out to the ranch. And no decent man would dare ask. As badly as he'd like to find a place to sleep for the night, he knew Miss Worthington couldn't afford to rent a room, and he was loath to leave her alone.

"Well. . ." Her shoulders trembled as she took a shaky breath. She turned to him, her lips curving into a half smile. "Be careful not to overexert yourself until that gash heals. And you, um, might want to get out your hanky. You seem to be bleeding again."

He fished out his handkerchief and pressed it to his temple.

"Good-bye, Mr. Chance. Thank you for your kindness earlier." She walked away. Heart in his throat, Titus watched her go, trying desperately to think of a way to make her stay.

"Miss Worthington." He hurried to join her.

"Yes?"

Gulping like a schoolboy who, for the very first time, figures out that girls aren't a nuisance, Titus clenched his hat tightly. "It would be my honor if you would accompany me inside for a meal." Holding his breath, he awaited her answer, all the while allowing his mind to think ahead.

Her eyebrows pushed together into a deep frown. "I appreciate your kindness, Mr. Chance, but I cannot accept charity." She gave a stubborn jerk of her chin. The show of dignity shot like an arrow, piercing Titus's heart. The tremor in her bottom lip as she desperately fought for control beckoned to be kissed away. Though everything in him begged to comply, he knew better.

Charity. She thought that was what he was offering? How did he tell her that he'd been born the moment he looked into her eyes? That the sky was bluer, the air fresher? That all he could think about was her beautiful, fawn-like eyes and silky auburn hair?

She cleared her throat, and he realized he'd been staring. "Good-bye, Mr. Chance. Once again, thank you for your kindness.

Knowing it was now or never, Titus gently took hold of her arm. "Miss Worthington, I would never insult you by implying you would accept charity." He pressed his hat over his heart. "The truth is, I'd love the chance to repay *your* kindness."

She hesitated, the lamplight reflecting the doubt in her eyes.

"Humor me? Please?"

A smile played across her lips. "All right, Mr. Chance. You've talked me into it."

Relief flooded him. For the next hour and a half he would enjoy her company, during which time he would try to figure out a way to help a woman who refused to take charity.

≈

Alisa was forced to use all her restraint not to slurp the delicious vegetable soup or wolf down warm slices of buttered bread. Slowly, much too slowly, her stomach began to lose the empty ache that had plagued her for two days and two nights. She ventured a glance at Mr. Chance. The gash on his temple still didn't look too good. "How's that feeling?" she asked.

"I guess if I said, 'Like I'd been shot,' you'd just think I was trying to make you laugh again."

Laughter bubbled from her.

"Ah, and I see it worked."

She'd never met anyone quite like Mr. Chance. A smart, funny man with a heart of gold. She wasn't so silly as to think he really had asked her to dinner to repay her kindness. He knew she was famished and had no money. So far God had taken care of her, but even she knew that she couldn't allow Mr. Chance to do anything else for her. Not only was it not proper, but it simply wasn't fair of her to presume upon his good nature. But she had a suspicion that he felt responsible for her. Though the thought sent a thrill from her heart straight down to her toes, she knew she had to relieve him of that sense of duty before it went too far.

Just as she opened her mouth to insist they part company as soon as they finished their meal, the door opened.

A muffled groan came from Mr. Chance's side of the table. She arched her brow and stared at him a moment. He sipped his milk but stared at the door over the rim of his glass. Alisa followed his gaze and almost gasped. A young woman with ringlets of blond hair that didn't look entirely real sashayed into the room ahead of an older couple. She worked the room like a politician, nodding to the men who sat around the four long tables. Every eye watched her, and as far as Alisa could tell, the young woman enjoyed the attention. She batted her lashes and touched shoulders as she passed. Then her eyes lit on Titus. And Alisa. All merriment fled her expression. Her face turned three shades of red, and her green eyes narrowed to slits. She looked like a cat about to pounce.

"Oh, no," Mr. Chance muttered. "She's coming over."

"Why, Titus, sweetheart, this is quite a surprise."

Titus stood. "Hello, Priscilla. We just got off the stage from San Francisco and decided to get a bite."

"Sit down and eat, you silly goose." She turned to Alisa, and her ruby lips—was that stained on?—curved into a sly smile. "He's such a gentleman."

Like a queen granting favors, she offered Alisa a slight nod of her head. "I'm Priscilla White. My parents are over there talking with some of the old folks in town. We own the dry goods store. And you are?"

Alisa hesitated. She glanced at Titus, who looked as perplexed as she felt. "Alisa Worthington." Loving the sound of her name, Alisa smiled.

"Titus, darling, aren't you going to ask me to sit down? I must admit I am totally famished. Mother ordered me an entire new wardrobe, and it arrived today. From New York! I plumb wore myself out trying things on." She motioned to the ridiculous pink gown she wore. "Do you like it, Titus? I know you love me to wear pink."

"Uh, yeah. Prissy. And do sit down."

Alisa's heart sank for two reasons. One. This woman obviously had a claim to Mr. Chance. And two. Nothing about Mr. Chance so far in their short acquaintance had indicated that he had such bad taste. Alisa locked in on his gaze. He spoke a silent apology with those warm blue eyes. But some things were beyond apologies. Extending a dinner invitation when one has a prior commitment to another girl, for instance. She glared at him and sniffed her disdain. If she'd been strong enough, she'd have left the plate of chicken, potatoes, and fresh garden peas and told him, "No, thank you." But her mouth watered at the sight and smell of the wonderful food, so she picked up her fork instead. The nightmare in fake ringlets and frightful pink spoke faster than an auctioneer, paying very little attention to Alisa.

So Alisa shoveled bite after bite into her mouth, making no attempt to follow the conversation.

"And where are you from, Miss Worthington?"

Alisa nearly choked. She glanced up from her plate, met the catlike gaze, and chewed hard. The silence at the table seemed palpable as she swallowed down the bite with a gulp of milk.

Sensing the other girl's impatience, Alisa couldn't help but prolong the silence a bit. Deliberately, she dabbed her mouth with her napkin. "I'm sorry. What was the question?"

A longsuffering sigh blew from Priscilla's lips—which Alisa was now convinced were painted. "I simply asked where you're from."

"San Francisco."

"And what, may I ask, are you doing in our quaint little town?"

Calling this dusty hole-in-the-wall a town was a bit of a stretch, but "quaint" was absolutely laughable. Still, the girl had her. What could she possibly say? *My father accused me of killing my grandmother and I narrowly escaped imprisonment by running away?*

Though she couldn't explain why she did it, Alisa found herself glancing at Mr. Chance for support. He caught her gaze, and the shining armor began to sparkle in the light of the lamp.

He cleared his throat, looked Priscilla squarely in the eyes, and said, "Miss Worthington is coming to work at the ranch."

four

Titus had set a new record. This was the first time in his life he'd ever made two women gasp in horror simultaneously.

"Whatever do you mean, she will be working at the ranch?" Prissy's eyes had narrowed dangerously. "Miss *Worthington* hardly looks like a ranch hand to me."

Miss Worthington's face turned deep red, and the question in her eyes echoed Prissy's concern.

Clearing his throat, Titus glanced from one bewildered woman to the other. "Miriam could use the help. She has a pretty heavy workload with all of us men plus Daniel's two youngsters."

Finding her voice before Prissy could jump in, Miss Worthington managed to croak, "I don't understand."

A smug look flitted across Prissy's face, and Titus knew she'd caught him in his—if not a lie, then definitely—stretch of the truth. It was obvious Miss Worthington was hearing about her new job for the first time.

"That's right. I never got around to explaining things to Miss Worthington."

Prissy's haughty expression faded to one of humility.

"I should say you didn't." Miss Worthington's frown spoke for itself, compelling Titus to speak up quickly before she could ruin his developing plan. Why *not* hire Miss Worthington? Miriam could certainly use the help. And he'd rather chew off his arm than leave Miss Worthington to the mercy of the slew of fellas staring at her from around the four neighboring tables.

"Miss Worthington," he appealed to her, hoping she'd take the hint and simmer down while he explained.

She scowled and sent him an all-right-but-make-it-good expression, folding her arms for emphasis.

"Okay, it's like this. My brother Daniel lost his wife in childbirth almost two years ago."

"Oh, I'm so sorry."

"Thank you. Anyway, Miriam showed up a few months later, not knowing her sister had passed on. Daniel and Gideon wanted to send her right back, but we all voted that her cooking was the best we'd ever tasted, and besides, Polly and Ginny Mae needed a woman's care."

"Polly and Ginny Mae?"

Titus grinned at the very thought of his young nieces. "Daniel's girls. Polly's four, and Ginny Mae's not yet two."

"I see." She chewed her bottom lip and stared at the table as though trying to gather the information into something that made sense. "I'm afraid I don't understand—"

"The fact of the matter is that Gideon snatched up Miriam pretty quick and married her before the circuit-riding preacher left to take on his own pastorate. But there are an awful lot of us out there for one woman. This is a rough land and really not fitting for a woman. At least not one alone on a ranch with. . .all of us."

"Oh, honestly, Titus." Prissy's outburst reminded him of her presence. She turned to Alisa. "What he's trying to say is that those brothers of his are utter ruffians. Miriam has done wonders taming Gideon, but there are just too many of them for her to handle alone."

She turned back to Titus as though he should thank her.

How could he have ever thought he wanted to marry such an indelicate woman? For all her pink and ribbons and lace, Prissy White had the manners of a bawling calf, and up close to another woman, she wasn't even all that pretty. That fancy finishing school she'd attended back East had been a colossal waste of time and money. But that was none of his business. He was just thanking the Lord that she'd turned down his proposal. Now he was free to court. . .

"Miss Worthington. Perhaps I was a mite deceptive in letting on like you were already coming to the ranch to work, but truth be told, we need all the help we can get. We can't pay much, but you'd have a roof over your head and plenty of food."

She hesitated, averting her gaze to her clasped fingers. "I don't know. . . ."

"I can assure you there's nothing improper at our house. We're God-fearing folks. Even hold the Sunday meetings at our ranch. So you have nothing to worry about."

The door crashed open. Miss Worthington jumped as a wolf whistle blistered the air. "Looky there, Logan. Titushhh brung us another woman. Gideon got the lasssht purty girl, but I got dibs on thisssh one."

Titus's stomach dropped at the sight of Miss Worthington's bewildered, accusing glare.

His two brothers staggered up to the table, obviously inebriated. "Hiya, Titus," Logan said, pounding Titus's back until it felt bruised. "Shhhaw the stage come in. Wuz you on it?"

Titus shot to his feet, snagging each young man by the collar.

"Hey!"

"Whachhhha doin', Titusshhh?"

"I can't believe you two have been drinking. If there weren't a couple of ladies present, I'd thrash you good. Right here and now."

"Awww, Titushhh."

Titus's anger hit him on two levels. One, the boys hadn't touched a drop in months. And two, by the look of utter horror on Miss Worthington's face, no amount of cajoling was going to convince her to come work at the ranch.

"Why, Titus," Prissy said, poorly concealed amusement dripping from her painted lips. "Aren't you going to introduce Miss Worthington to your brothers? After all, she *will* be helping to take care of your wonderful *God-fearing* family." With a triumphant laugh, she stood. "So very nice to meet you, Miss Worthington. Don't worry. There are plenty of men in town who will offer you marriage. A single woman in Reliable doesn't stay single for long, unless she's choosy." She gave Titus a pointed look. The boys hee-hawed.

"Be quiet," Titus ordered, tightening his hold on each collar. "Do you two have the buckboard?"

" 'Courshh. Miriam shhhhent usssh for supplies."

"Good. Get to it. Stay there, and wait for me."

"We're shhhorry, Titushh," Logan slurred. "It'll never happen agin."

"Yeah, we promishhh."

"Well, you should be ashamed. Miriam sent you to town in good faith that you'd behave yourselves. How do you think she'll feel when she finds out you've been hanging out at the Nugget? And you've upset Miss Worthington."

"Aw, Missshhhh W. . .wor. . .Misshhh, please accept my apolozhyyy." Bryce bent at the waist, trying to be gallant, and pitched forward. He caught himself just before falling into her lap—which Titus knew from experience was a wondrous thing. Still, he didn't want the boy, or any other man, for that matter, knowing it firsthand.

"You two go on to the wagon. I'll be there soon."

The boys staggered back across the room and left the diner, banging the door behind them.

Rarely did Titus feel nervous, but there was no denying the trembling in his gut as he dared to meet Miss Worthington's gaze. She arched a brow. Titus recognized the challenge. She'd let him explain but wasn't promising to believe a word he said.

"All right. Logan and Bryce are the youngest of us six brothers."

"I thought you said you were a God-fearing family." Miss Worthington's voice remained soft and calm. Again, Titus felt optimism rise.

"They got a little rowdy last year until our older brother Gideon threatened to tan their hides if he ever caught them at it again." He glanced in the direction his younger brothers had gone, then looked back to Miss Worthington. "I don't know what's gotten into them to end up at the Nugget again after such a long time."

"The Nugget?"

Titus cringed. "The saloon."

"Do you really need help for your sister-in-law, or were you only trying to keep me from being humiliated in front of your girl?"

Titus started. "First of all, yes. Miriam needs help, and I'd be obliged if you'd consider coming to work on the ranch. Second, Prissy White is not my girl. Not really."

"Not really?"

"Well, I asked her to marry me, but she was considering a few other proposals at the time. I guess my pockets weren't deep enough for her."

"All right, Mr. Chance. I do need a job, and I'm used to large numbers to feed and care for. So I suppose I will accept your offer."

Titus nodded, aware of the curious stares coming from everyone in the room. "Will you consider the boys as proper chaperones? The ranch is an hour's ride east of here. No one in these parts would consider you compromised. But if it makes you uncomfortable, I'll make other arrangements for you."

Again her expression revealed her conflicting emotions. No doubt she realized she had no place to sleep but weighed that reality against the fact that night had fallen in earnest and she would be forced to ride with three strange men, two of whom were inebriated.

Gathering a shaky breath, she nodded. "I suppose they'll have to do."

Relief rushed over him like an ocean wave.

"I'm in your debt."

"No, Mr. Chance." She spoke so softly, he had to strain to hear.

Titus's heart leapt to his throat. "No?"

She kept her gaze steady on his. "We are both well aware that the debt owed is mine. Not yours."

❧

Despite her nervousness, Alisa couldn't help but gather a deep breath and drink in the fresh smell of pine wafting from the trees lining each side of the well-worn path. Nighttime usually frightened her, but out here the black sky shaded with rolling gray clouds appeared like a painting created by a master. The fragrance of the coming rain hung in the air.

Calm slowly replaced her jitters. She cut her gaze to Mr. Chance. He stared ahead, watching the road. Her stomach turned a flip just observing his profile. Black stubble formed a pattern across his jaw. To Alisa, the unshaven roughness only added to his good looks. As though unaware of the effect he was having on her, Mr. Chance absently hummed "Shall We Gather at the River," his rich baritone adding to the pleasure of being in his company.

He turned his head as though aware of her perusal. A smile curved his full lips, and Alisa had trouble looking away. "Everything okay?" he asked.

"Yes." Cheeks burning, she forced herself to stare ahead into the darkness.

He jerked his thumb toward the back of the wagon. "Listen to those two."

The two lanky boys snored happily. She knew they wouldn't be so happy when they awoke, and she took satisfaction from it. "Perhaps their condition in the morning will discourage them from indulging in spirits." Her cheeks burned as she realized she'd spoken her musings aloud. What would he think of her even knowing about headaches and sick stomachs—consequences of too much alcohol?

"I hope so. Only the Lord can deliver a person from a hankering for the temporary pleasures of sin."

Impressed with his astute observation and obvious love for the Lord, Alisa began to feel much more at ease. "How is your head feeling, Mr. Chance?"

"Well, let's just say, I probably won't be in any better shape than those two in the morning, but at least I got mine honestly."

Alisa gave a soft laugh then sobered as she realized that Mr.

Chance had been stolen from. "Will you go to the sheriff?"

He nodded. "Mr. Wayne will also inform the marshal in San Francisco."

"I hope you get your horse back."

His smile nearly stole her breath. "That's sweet of you, Alisa."

Alisa started at his use of her given name.

"Do you object to being called that? I won't do it if you feel it's inappropriate."

"N. . .no, of course you may use my name. I will be a servant in your house, after all."

Without speaking, he tugged the reins, and the horses stopped. He turned to give her his full attention. "Look at me," he ordered.

Alisa did as he commanded, meeting his stern gaze. "I want you to get that notion out of your head right now."

"N. . .notion? I thought I would be working for you."

"Well. . ." He hesitated, then scowled deeply. "You'll be helping Miriam and will be compensated for it, but that doesn't make you a servant."

"It doesn't?"

"No," he growled.

"Then what does it make me?" Alisa fought the giggle rising in her at his discomfiture.

"Part of the family."

"You marryin' her, Titus?"

"Shut up and go back to sleep, Logan," Mr. Chance growled. "I'm trying to explain to Miss Worthington that she isn't a servant."

" 'K," he mumbled and resumed snoring.

"Alisa. . .Miss Worthington. . ."

Alisa decided to quell his discomfort. She placed her palm on his arm then lifted it off again when his muscle twitched. "I know what you mean. I appreciate your generosity. Please do call me Alisa, as it will be much easier if we are to see each other often."

"We'll most definitely be seeing each other." His eyes searched hers, and he smiled, once again revealing straight healthy teeth. "Every breakfast, lunch, and supper." His lazy, husky voice created pleasing word pictures. Warmth slithered across her belly at the thought. "During family devotions, long walks by the creek, Sunday meetings."

"Picnicsshhh. I like picnicsshhh."

He glared over the seat. "Mind your own business, Bryce."

Still tingling from the moment that had just passed between them, Alisa released the laughter bubbling up, grateful for the opportunity to ease the tension.

"Well, I suppose we should get moving, anyway."

Alisa nodded. Pins of nervous energy pricked at her spine. Would the rest of the family welcome her? If not, where would she go? She'd be right back in the same situation she was in before Mr. Chance came into her life. Only this time. . .this time she wouldn't have a champion.

five

Alisa tilted her head to one side like a curious puppy and stared at the group of buildings in front of her as Titus pulled the reins and the wagon halted. "It's like a small town," she said in amazement.

Titus's low, throaty chuckle pulled her attention from the view.

"How many brothers did you say you have?"

"We're a close bunch." He pointed toward the structures. "On the left is the main cabin. Gideon and Miriam live there, and that's also where we share our meals. Next is my cabin. We built it for Miriam, but when she and Giddy married, I took over. Next to that, those two knuckleheads in back bunk together. My brother Paul has the next cabin. I used to bunk with him. And up there on the far right is my brother Daniel's cabin. He's the one with the two little girls."

"It's wonderful you have such a large, close family."

He cocked his head and gave her a lazy grin. "It's not always wonderful. But usually it is. We don't want to split up the land, but we knew we'd need our privacy as each of us marries. Besides, Daniel keeps us in logs."

"One man cut down the trees to build all of this?"

"Pretty much. After his wife died, he needed something to occupy him so that he didn't go crazy. Felling the trees seemed to be his way of working things out."

Pity warmed Alisa's heart. "I understand."

Titus looked at her sharply. "My brothers are going to be curious about a woman traveling alone with no extra money or even a change of clothes. Do you feel like you want to tell me your story?"

"I. . .don't think I can just yet."

Not until she was certain he would believe her and not send her back to San Francisco to be arrested for her grandmother's murder.

Her grandmother.

"I understand." He climbed down and headed to the back of the wagon. "Hey, knuckleheads. Wake up."

Alisa's mind moved past the grumblings and mumblings of the drunken young men. For at least the thousandth time in the past two days, she shook her head to rekindle the memory of her dear grandmother's words. She truly wasn't alone. Or she wouldn't have been if Robert Worthington had been the sort of father a girl could be proud of. Growing up, she'd always thought if one had money, that person must be truly above all others in manners and grace. After all, would God reward someone who was truly wicked? But her father had certainly proven her wrong.

She shuddered at the memory of his steely, hate-ridden glare as he accused her. Despite his wonderful mother, some-how cords of evil had slithered around his heart and squeezed the decency from him. For the first time, Alisa understood that the love of money could, indeed, be a root of all evil. She'd almost rather have no father than to have one who was wicked. But that hadn't been her choice, and now because her dream of finding a family had been granted, she had to run to escape the injustice of being falsely accused.

Before she could succumb to ready tears, Alisa noticed that

Titus was at her side of the wagon, holding his hand out to help her down.

28.

Titus swallowed hard as he approached the door. Alisa's warm hand tucked in the crook of his arm made it difficult for him to think, let alone formulate a logical reason that he hired a girl to help Miriam without a family vote. He could imagine the backlash.

Alisa released a shaky breath, the first sign she'd displayed that she was less than confident. Titus covered her hand. "Don't worry. Miriam will love you."

With a barely perceptible nod, she squeezed his arm. "I'll be all right."

"Let's go in." He knocked on the door of the main cabin. Miriam appeared in short order. She smiled broadly when she saw him. "Titus, I'm so glad you made it back." Then she seemed to notice Alisa. Rather than asking questions, she opened the door wider. "Come in, please. Your guest looks worn to a frazzle."

Alisa's lips curved into a weary smile. "Thank you."

Gideon stood when Alisa entered—manners compliments of his new wife—and offered her his chair at the table. "Please, have a seat." He held her chair and stared at Titus over her head. His expression clearly spoke his disapproval and his curiosity.

Titus cleared his throat, suddenly aware of the silence in the room. Silence he was expected to fill. "I'd like you both to meet Alisa Worthington. Alisa, this is my brother Gideon and his wife, Miriam." So that took care of the names.

"And where did you meet Titus, Miss Worthington?" Miriam's pleasant voice broke through the silence.

God bless Miriam.

"On the stage from San Francisco."

Titus inwardly cringed at the next obvious question.

"Oh? And what brings you to Reliable?"

Alisa's gaze faltered, and a pretty blush crept to her cheeks.
"I. . .well. . ."

"I hired her to help Miriam."

"What?"

"How thoughtful!"

Gideon and Miriam spoke as one then looked at each other.
Alisa glanced from one to the other, then to Titus. He nodded, hoping to reassure her, but from the crestfallen expression
clouding her face, he knew he'd fallen abysmally short of
accomplishing his goal.

"Miss Worthington, you must be dead on your feet,"
Miriam said. "Have you eaten supper?"

Alisa nodded. "At the station in Reliable."

"Well, how about coming with me? I'll get you tucked into
my bed. You can sleep with me tonight."

Gideon choked on a sip of coffee. "What?"

Miriam smiled sweetly at her husband. "You and Titus have
some talking to do, and Miss Worthington looks just about
ready to fall asleep sitting up."

Titus had to fight the urge to slap his brother on the back
and laugh out loud. But Alisa's concerned voice halted him.

"Please, don't put your husband out for my sake. I can
sleep anywhere. The floor is perfectly fine. I've done it plenty
of times."

Alarm seized Titus, and he wanted to pound Gideon for
not being more gracious. Who was Alisa that, by her own
admission, she'd slept on the floor plenty of times?

At Miriam's loud clearing of the throat, Gideon's face grew bright red. "Like Miriam said, my brothers and I have some talking to do tonight."

"About me?"

Titus grinned and waited to see how his brother would respond.

"Yes, Miss Worthington."

The smile she displayed was so sweet, Titus wanted to sweep her up in his arms and protect her from all the heartache she'd suffered. Wanted to kiss away the trembling of her lips, the worry in her eyes. "I understand, Mr. Chance," she said to Gideon. She lifted her gaze to Titus. "I'll not hold you to your offer. You've been more than generous, and I appreciate your kindness more than I can express."

Anger burned in Titus. "You're staying." He glared at Gideon. "She's staying. Vote or no vote. Even if I have to marry her. She's not going anywhere."

Silence thickened the air. Alisa pushed back her chair and stood. She faced Titus, her face white. "If your brothers vote against my employment here, I'll leave without a fuss. But make no mistake. No man *has* to marry me."

"That's not what I—"

Miriam stepped forward. "How about if you two go on and call the boys to a meeting?" She rose to her tiptoes and kissed her husband soundly on the mouth. "Be sure to invite God's opinion in this decision."

Gideon nodded, cupping her cheek. The love flowing between them made Titus's heart ache as it always did. He wanted that feeling. With Alisa, he was closer to it than he'd ever been before. And now like an idiot, he'd somehow insulted her and had most likely lost her before she was even his.

"Let's go." Gideon clapped him on the shoulder.

Shaking off his brother's hand, Titus reached out to touch Alisa's arm. "Wait a second, Alisa. Let me explain."

"Explanations aren't necessary," she murmured.

Miriam looked at him with silent appeal. "I'll cook you some flapjacks in the morning, Titus. We have fresh honey and strawberry preserves. But for now, why don't you go?"

With a final glance at Alisa's crumpled face, Titus nodded.

"Don't worry," Miriam said for his ears only. "I'll take good care of her. You concentrate on swinging the vote in your favor. I have a feeling Alisa's been through a rough time and needs us."

❧

"Great hoppy toads, this looks good, Miriam!"

Alisa's eyes popped open at the sound of voices in the other room. Light streamed into the room, blinding her for a moment.

"You boys hush before you wake up Miss Worthington," Miriam hissed.

Alisa smiled. After a refreshing sponge bath, she'd changed into a borrowed nightgown and had been asleep practically before her head hit the pillow. Now she knew she must be frightfully late to breakfast, but her muscles ached so badly from the past two days' activities that she couldn't bring herself to hop right out of bed and face the day.

"When do you think the new gal's gonna wake up?"

Alisa's ears perked to the sound.

"Wish I could remember what she looks like. Titus says she's just about the prettiest thing he's ever seen."

He did? Alisa's heart thrilled to the information.

"Well, I like that!" Miriam's teasing voice filtered through the thin wall.

"Well, he didn't mean nothin' by it, Miriam. I think he's smitten, that's all."

This conversation was getting better and better. She'd certainly awakened at just the right moment.

The only question on her heart and in her mind was whether or not she would be allowed to stay. Spurred on by the thought, she pushed back the quilt and swung her legs over the side of the bed. For certain she wouldn't be hired if her potential employers thought she couldn't even get out of bed at a decent time in the morning.

"So, when do you reckon she'll get up?"

"You asked that already, Logan."

Her gown was gone. Panic swelled her throat. She had laid the dress across the chair last night. Now it was gone. Whatever was she to do? Shoulders slumped, she sat back on the bed and listened to the conversation coming from the other room.

"I don't remember what she looks like."

Something clattered, and the sound of boot steps clacked brusquely across the wooden floor. Miriam's voice sounded sharp and firm. "You would if you hadn't imbibed. I'm so ashamed."

"We're sorry, Miriam. But sometimes when his friends want to socialize, a man just can't help it."

"A man of character can always help it. God promised we would not be tempted beyond our ability to do the right thing. So spare me your excuses."

Respect for the woman rose inside of Alisa. Suddenly she desperately wanted to be allowed to stay. Her stomach quivered at the thought of a vote against her. She slid to her knees and rested her elbows on the bed. Sometimes her heart felt so full, she couldn't form the words beyond, "Oh, please." And now she found her vocabulary once more limited to those words. "Please, dear Jesus. Oh, please, please let me stay." Slowly, the pounding of her longing heart slowed to normal, and she rested her cheek against the back of her hand.

In a stranger's room, peace flooded her soul, and the words of entreaty became words of praise. "I thank Thee for giving me a name. For taking care of me so far." The fact was, she didn't have to stay at Chance Ranch for God to meet her needs. Whether He chose for her to leave or stay, her heart calmed to the fact that He was well able to take care of her. With a smile, she gathered a deep breath and opened her eyes.

Whatever happened. God was in control.

six

Robert Worthington surveyed the two-story frame home critically as his boots clicked on the cobblestone walk. Paint was cracked and peeling off just about every board. He gave two solid raps on the door. A moment later, a girl of perhaps ten years appeared.

"May I help you?"

"I'm looking for the woman who runs this place."

"Would you like to come in?"

"Yes. Thank you."

The child stepped aside. "I'll tell Mrs. Perryman you're here."

Robert looked around at the dingy furniture, chipped tables, and worn curtains and rugs. His daughter had grown up in this dump? He pushed aside the thought as soon as it came. No. She wasn't his daughter. Alisa was the unfortunate result of a few nights of fun on his part. She never should have been found.

Anger burned within his breast as it did whenever Alisa's heart-shaped face and innocent brown eyes came to his mind. Why should he lose everything to a daughter he'd never wanted in the first place?

The sound of footsteps captured his attention, pulling him from his thoughts. An attractive, middle-aged woman smiled as she entered, followed by the young girl. A girl who might have been Alisa a few years ago. He shook the thought from his mind and scowled. The woman cocked her head to the side, the twinkle in her green eyes replaced with caution.

"May I help you?"

"You run this place?"

"I'm Mrs. Perryman. Yes. I care for the children. Are you looking for a child to adopt?"

Robert recoiled at the thought. "No!"

"I see." She turned to the girl. "Sarah, please let the children know to continue with their lessons."

"You teach them here? Why do they not attend public school?"

"Children can be cruel. Most of these children find they prefer to be taught at home."

Robert shrugged off the concern. Why should he care if a bunch of orphans received a proper education or not? He was here for one reason only. To find Alisa.

"I'm looking for my daughter. I believe you raised her here."

The woman's eyes lit up. "You've traced your child to us? This will be the second family reunion this year."

Realizing she was talking about Alisa, Robert felt his ears burn. "To tell you the truth, Mrs. Perryman, Alisa is my daughter."

Confusion clouded her face. "Perhaps you'd better come into the kitchen, and you can explain over a cup of tea."

"Really, that won't be. . ." Robert sighed as she turned and headed down the hallway. All he wanted was information, not a tea party, but he followed her swishing gray skirts, nostalgia filling him at the familiar sound. There were times when he missed his mother so badly his throat ached. Unpredictable moments such as this. He cleared his throat to ease the tightness.

"Is Alisa missing, Mr. Worthington?" she asked over her shoulder.

"Yes."

She opened the door to the kitchen and entered, stepping aside as she waited for Robert to follow. He did.

"Please have a seat at the table while I prepare our tea." She moved to the stove with a quiet grace and began preparing a kettle of water.

Robert sat in the chair she'd indicated. The wood felt wobbly beneath him, and he wondered if it would hold his weight. "It seems there are plenty of things around here in need of repair."

She sighed, pumping water into the kettle. "I'm afraid you're right. Since Mr. Perryman passed on four years ago, I haven't been able to keep up with much. Some of the boys are handy with tools and can help with repairs, as long as the jobs don't require funds we simply don't have."

Robert knew she wasn't hinting. But he knew how to play a situation to his advantage all the same. "How many children do you care for here?" First rule of thumb when trying to weasel something out of a person—make them think you care.

She turned to him and smiled. "Right now we have seven boys ranging in age from four to sixteen. And ten girls approximately the same ages." She took in a slow breath. "Unfortunately, Seth, my oldest boy, will have to be moving on soon."

She sounded so sad, Robert was prompted to ask, "Why is that?"

"Once they reach the age where they are able to find work, we must make room for new children. It breaks my heart to see them go. I was little more than the oldest among them myself when we started the orphanage. But they understand, and most come back often to visit. Some even help out. Alisa always brought her pay over here. I tried to protest, but she left it with one of the children when I refused to take it."

She poured the tea and set a chipped cup in front of him, along with a creamer. "I'm afraid I don't have any sugar at the moment. Little Judith turned eight yesterday, and I used the last of it to bake a cake."

"Plain is fine." Robert detested the way his heart constricted at anyone being so poor as to make a choice between having sugar for tea or using the last to bake a cake. He gathered himself together. All the more reason for her to take him up on his forthcoming offer.

"Mrs. Perryman. I can see you care deeply for these. . . orphans."

"You see correctly." She stirred a drop of cream into her cup. "My husband and I were never blessed with children of our own. The children God brings to us. . .to me. . .become part of a family. Now what of Alisa? We missed her yesterday for Judith's birthday."

Armed with confidence, Robert flashed a smile. "I'm afraid she's run away."

A frown creased Mrs. Perryman's already wrinkled brow. "That doesn't sound like Alisa. Was she in danger?"

"Of course not. I'm afraid my mother passed on very recently and my. . .daughter took it rather hard."

"Oh, how sad." Her green eyes drew him in, and he almost forgot his objective. Almost. Not quite.

"Yes. Alisa and I are all the other has in the world now."

"How long has she been gone?"

"My mother passed away two nights ago. I haven't seen

Alisa since." Robert sipped the weak tea. "The reason I bothered you is that I hoped you'd seen her. I take it you haven't?"

"I'm afraid not. But if I do, I'll be sure to tell her you're looking for her."

Robert inwardly cringed. That would be the worst thing she could do. Alisa would run and never return if she knew he had come here to look for her. "There's more to it than that."

Mrs. Perryman frowned. "I don't understand."

"Alisa is under the impression she is somehow responsible for my mother's demise."

"However would she have gotten such an idea?"

"I'm as much at a loss about that as you are, Mrs. Perryman. But it's very, very important that I find her." He leaned forward, his hands wrapped around the teacup. "If Alisa contacts you, I would appreciate if you would send word immediately." He reached into his coat pocket and pulled out ten dollars.

Mrs. Perryman's eyes narrowed. She squared her shoulders. "Sir, if you are trying to pay me to betray Alisa, I would like you to leave my home this instant."

"Please, Mrs. Perryman. You misunderstand. I am simply donating to your cause."

"The Lord provides for our needs. We do not need your donation." The woman stood. "You may show yourself out."

Frustration shook Robert to the core. He looked toward the door and saw a dark head peeking around the corner.

"Come out here," he ordered.

Slowly a small boy moved to stand in front of him.

"What's your name?"

"Spencer." The freckles on his nose crunched together as he grinned, a wide, gap-toothed smile.

Robert found himself responding. He walked by, ruffled the

boy's head, and handed him the ten dollars. "Give this to Mrs. Perryman and tell her to buy some sugar. No strings attached."

He berated himself as he stalked down the walk away from the nearly dilapidated orphanage.

What kind of a fool was he?

ॐ

Titus felt his stomach respond to the smell of bacon frying and flapjacks staying warm in the oven. True to her word, Miriam had cooked all of his favorites. He scanned the room but didn't find Alisa present. His gaze traveled to Miriam. Her lips curved. "She's still asleep."

"Good. That was quite a stage ride yesterday. I'm sure she needs her rest."

"In the meantime, we can take our vote." Gideon kept his voice low.

"What vote?" Bryce reached for a flapjack then turned his gaze to Gideon.

"About Miss Worthington staying."

"Why do we need to vote on that? I figured she was staying."

Daniel wiped the jam from Ginny Mae's chin. "This life is too hard on a woman. I think we ought to do her a favor and send her back where she came from."

Frustration chewed at Titus. He raked his fingers through his unruly hair and glared at his widowed brother. "We're all sorry Hannah died, Daniel. But that doesn't mean no woman is cut out for this life. Alisa should have the right to decide for herself."

"You could always marry her like Gideon married Miriam," Logan suggested. Bryce passed him the plate of bacon. Logan's face blanched, and he shook his head.

"He's right," Bryce offered. "Then we wouldn't have any

choice but to let her stay."

Paul and Gideon cackled. "She already turned him down," Gideon informed them.

"All right." Miriam set another plate of flapjacks on the table. "If you don't lower your voices, you'll wake her up. Take the vote, and get it over with."

"We already know what Daniel thinks," Titus said.

Daniel grunted and gulped his coffee.

"I vote yes. Now can I go back to bed?" Logan held his head in his hands. "I'm not hungry."

"I vote yes, too." Bryce forked another flapjack. "If Logan's not eating, I'll take his."

Titus shook his head at his brother. So much for his morning pain teaching him a lesson.

"Paul?"

Paul sipped his coffee. "I haven't even met her yet. Where will she sleep? She can't stay with Miriam."

"You better believe she can't."

Miriam's face grew red at her husband's outburst.

"I have that all worked out," Titus said quickly. "How about if I move back in with you, Paul? Alisa can have my cabin."

Paul shrugged. "That'd be all right with me."

"So you vote yes?"

"I reckon so."

"That settles it then. We don't need Gideon's vote. We have a majority." Titus felt a smug grin tug at his mouth.

Miriam walked by and patted his shoulder. "Do I get a vote?"

No one said a word.

"After all. I'm part of the family now, too, aren't I?"

"Well, sure." Even if she voted no, the four of them had a majority. Titus smiled to encourage her.

"Well, of course I vote yes, but that isn't the point. From now on, I wish to be included in these decisions."

"Miriam's right," Gideon said. "She's an adult member of the family and deserves a voice when we vote."

"I think we should vote on whether Miriam should vote or not," Bryce said between bites.

Miriam sniffed and tossed a dish towel at him. "How about if I vote to stop cooking flapjacks just the way you like them?"

"Just kidding. I think Miriam should have a vote, too."

Gideon slapped him on the shoulder. "You'll agree to anything if it means the difference between Miriam's cooking or going back to Paul's."

"Can't say as I blame him," Paul said through a grin just before he shoveled another bite into his mouth.

"All right," Titus said with a nod. "Then we're agreed. Miss Worthington stays, and from now on, Miriam gets a vote."

Daniel grunted his disapproval but didn't speak.

Logan rose. "I'm going back to my cabin," he said a bit thinly. "You'll have to do without me today."

"Get some rest," Gideon said sternly. "But when you get up, we're going to have another talk about you two and your drinking."

Logan nodded and slunk toward the door.

"Then it's settled. Alisa stays." Titus glanced toward the other room, his stomach churning with anticipation at seeing her again.

"Someone's coming," Logan announced from the open door.

"Who?"

"Looks like Miss White."

All eyes turned to Titus. Bryce snickered. "Guess she wants to marry you after all."

seven

Alisa's heart sank at Bryce's theory about Prissy and her matrimonial intentions. Guilt pricked her that she'd been eavesdropping the whole time, but the truth was, she couldn't leave the room without clothes, and so far, hers hadn't materialized. She could only assume Miriam had taken them to be washed—which was sweet of her—but what would Alisa wear in the meantime?

She jumped a moment later when Miriam slipped into the room. The other woman's lips twitched. "I guess you heard the vote."

Warmth flooded Alisa's cheeks. She nodded.

"I took your dress to wash. But naturally it isn't dry yet. I brought you one of mine. You're a bit taller than I am, but it should work until yours is dry." Miriam deposited the clothing on the bed. "I see you tidied up in here. Thank you. You are going to be handy to have around."

Alisa smiled at the praise.

Miriam walked to her wardrobe and pulled out some white lacy articles. "You'll need these as well."

"Thank you."

"Just hurry and get yourself presentable. Prissy White just pulled up."

"I. . .I met her last night, I'm afraid. I. . .I don't mean, I'm afraid. I mean. . ." She cleared her throat. "Well, I made her acquaintance at dinner."

Miriam laughed. "It's all right. I completely understand. Prissy takes a little getting used to. Poor Titus."

"Poor Titus?"

"Obviously, Prissy's predatory nature took over when she saw you with him. She turned down his proposal—and she wasn't too nice about it—but it looks like she's changed her mind. It'll be interesting to see how Titus gets himself out of this bind."

"Why would he want to get out of it? If he asked her to marry him, he must love her." The very words left a bitter taste in Alisa's mouth.

Miriam waved her hands. "Nonsense. Love rarely has anything to do with marriage in these parts." A lovely smile tipped her lips. "There are exceptions of course. Anyway, I will admit Titus was smitten for a while. But that's all changed. I can see it in his eyes. You've definitely caused the glow of Prissy's presence to dim. He lights up like a Roman candle every time he looks at you."

Alisa tried not to allow her heartbeat to speed up. She couldn't put too much stock in a man whose heart switched allegiance so quickly. "I see."

If a man could get unsmitten with Prissy White that quickly, what was to say Titus Chance wouldn't meet a prettier face in a few days and get unsmitten with Alisa as well? A chuckle from Miriam pulled her back to the present. "Well, I'll go greet our guest while you get ready."

Alisa donned the underthings and the blue gown, which was slightly too short. After pulling her hair back into a loose chignon, a style her grandmother had mentioned was quite attractive, she stepped into the other room. All eyes turned to her, but she locked onto Titus's gaze and couldn't look away.

His smile started at his lips and spread upward until pleasure glowed in his eyes. "Good morning," he said, leaving Prissy's side and walking across the room to meet Alisa. He offered his arm. "May I escort you to breakfast? There's still plenty on the table. I could heat it up for you if you like."

A snort from Bryce brought a scowl to Titus's nearly perfect features.

Alisa felt her cheeks warm at his obvious attempt at. . . something. His gallantry wasn't lost on Prissy. The girl looked as though steam might blow from her ears at any second. Alisa took his arm and walked with him to the table. "Thank you, Titus. I'm sure the food is plenty warm."

"Would you like some coffee, Alisa?" Miriam asked.

"Yes, thank you."

"I'll get it," Titus offered.

"Perhaps I'll have a cup after all, Titus," Prissy said in a slightly falsetto voice.

"Uh, okay. Two cups of coffee coming right up."

Prissy flounced to the table and plopped down in the wooden chair next to Alisa. "Miriam," she said. "I'm surprised to see you doing all the work. I thought that's why Miss Worthington was hired."

Alisa gathered a steadying breath. She recognized the challenge and refused to take it up. She wouldn't embarrass herself by insulting her employer's guest.

Titus set two steaming cups on the table in front of Prissy and Alisa. "We're giving Alisa a day to rest from the stage ride and to get her bearings."

"Oh, of course. She must be exhausted. Poor dear." Prissy gave her the once over and then dismissed her. Alisa felt the slight to her toes, but again chose to let it go. As an orphan she had gained a lot of experience with once-over looks from townsfolk. She'd never been very good at swallowing the insults without resentment, but she had at least learned to keep her mouth shut.

She felt a warm hand squeeze her shoulder and looked up just as Titus moved around her to the end chair. "Did you sleep all right, Alisa?"

"I did." She smiled. "Thank you."

"Good!" He smiled back, and Alisa felt the background fade. They were the only two people in the cabin. "Today we'll get you all moved into my cabin."

A gasp from the ruffly, ribboned, pink-clad Prissy caused Alisa to jerk around. "Did you burn your mouth on the coffee, Miss White?"

"I am mortified that you will be sharing a cabin with my fiancé!" Prissy glared around the room, taking in the brothers and Miriam. "And quite frankly, I'm shocked that any of you would allow such an abomination."

Now it was Alisa's turned to gasp. She shot to her feet, knocking her coffee cup over in the process. The liquid made a brown trail toward Prissy's pink gown.

A scream escaped Prissy's painted lips as she tried in vain to jump up out of the way.

Alisa watched, horrified as the liquid trail met the fabric. Titus groaned. The rest of the men grunted with dread, and Miriam gasped. Prissy spun, her face red with fury. "You, you did that on purpose. You ruined my new gown from New York."

"I most certainly did not do it on purpose," Alisa said, fighting to keep her temper in check and respond quietly. *A soft answer turneth away wrath,* she reminded herself.

"You did too, you immoral girl." Prissy's hand shot out, landing across Alisa's cheek with a resounding *smack* and an explosion of pain. Alisa stepped back, palm over the stinging area. The girl's hand came up again. Too stunned to defend herself, Alisa watched the hand descend.

Titus stepped forward, grabbing Prissy's hand before she could strike a second time. "That's enough, Priscilla."

Tears pooled in her eyes. "Did you see what she did, Titus? She poured her coffee on my new gown on purpose. She's afraid you'll come back to me and turn her out."

"Don't be foolish," he ground out. "Miss Worthington will not be sharing the cabin with me, and I can't believe you'd think so little of me as to even entertain the notion."

"But you said—"

"I'm moving out of the cabin, and Miss Worthington will occupy it alone, of course."

Her trembling lips curved upward into a pouty smile. "What a relief. I was afraid she had corrupted you."

"Miss Worthington is completely devoted to her Christian faith. So you have no need to fear the corruption of my morals at her hands."

Humiliated by the entire conversation, Alisa stepped back. "Excuse me, please." Unable to meet anyone's gaze, she fled out the front door, around the house, and toward a path cut through the woods. As an orphan, she'd been ridiculed and falsely accused often, but never had she been accused of loose morals. The spiteful woman.

❧

Titus dropped Prissy's wrist and stomped outside in pursuit of Alisa. How could he ever have imagined himself in love with that frilly, flouncy, spiteful young woman? Standing next to

Alisa's quiet grace, Prissy was obviously inferior in quality of character. He certainly didn't want her to be the mother of his children.

Remembering Miriam's bout with poison oak last summer and her subsequent weeklong recovery, he hurried along the path behind the house, hoping Alisa would stay away from the woods.

If she stayed on the path, she'd come to the creek and be forced to wade or stop. He figured she'd stop. He was right. After a few more yards, he came to the clearing. Alisa stood along the bank of the creek, her arms wrapped around her.

A twig snapped beneath his feet. She turned her head at the sound.

Tenderness swelled Titus's heart at her red-rimmed eyes and tear-streaked cheeks. He went to her quickly and wrapped her in his arms without asking permission. Times like this called for comforting, and he didn't have to be an expert on women to realize his arms would be welcome.

She wilted against him, her head resting on his chest. Her arms were tucked between them. And while Titus might have preferred to have them wrapped around him, he understood her need to be cuddled. "Shhh. Honey. Everything is going to work out fine."

He stroked her silken hair, wishing it was loose and flowing instead of pulled back into a knot at the nape of her neck.

"What if she goes back to town, telling tales?"

"Who's she going to tell them to?"

"What do you mean?"

"Honey, this isn't San Francisco. There are only three decent women in Reliable, four if you count Prissy. You know that. The men aren't going to cotton to a woman's gossip."

She stayed in his arms, but he could feel her relaxing against him. When she pulled away, he took her chin between his thumb and forefinger and gently forced her to look up at him. Her lovely brown eyes were wide and innocent, filled with unshed tears. Her moist lips still trembled. Titus swallowed hard, fighting for control. Instinctively he knew kissing her would be a disastrous move.

"If it'll make you feel better, we could get married." The words came out of nowhere, sending a jolt through him.

She drew a sharp breath and stepped back.

"Titus?" Prissy's falsetto voice rang from the trail.

Alisa's eyes crinkled with amusement. "Don't you think you have enough fiancées for now?"

"Prissy's not my. . ."

"Oh, thank goodness. There you are."

"Yes," Alisa said, with a smirk. "Here he is. If you two will excuse me. I'd best go see if I can help Miriam clean up." She gave Prissy a sidelong glance as she walked by. "It's never too early to start earning my keep."

Prissy's sniff was the only response. Titus felt as though a cloud had drifted across the sun as he watched Alisa walk away. The warmth of her slender body wrapped in his arms filled him with a longing to go after her and tell her he was serious about the proposal. Out here it didn't matter if he'd only known her for a couple of days. They were both single adults. The attraction between them couldn't be denied. He frowned. Or maybe he was only assuming Alisa wasn't already spoken for. She hadn't seemed to even consider his proposal. Titus grimaced. How could he have blurted it out like that? This was the second time in less than twenty-four hours he'd suggested marrying her. The first time he'd made her angry.

This time, he'd amused her. She must think he threw out proposals at the drop of a hat.

Prissy's touch on his arm brought him back to the annoying situation at hand. "Titus, please. The ground is so soft from last night's rain, my heels keep digging in. I'll need you to carry me back to the wagon."

Was she serious?

Her lips trembled, but rather than tempting him to move in for a kiss as Alisa's had moments before, Prissy's lips made Titus recoil.

He softened when her eyes filled with real tears. "Please, Titus. My gown is already ruined. Mother's going to be fit to be tied as it is. I. . .I only came out to see you. To tell you that I. . ."

Dread clenched his gut. Then sympathy filled him as he observed her gown. A large coffee stain covered the skirt, and the bottom edge was wet and covered with mud.

"It's all right. Tell your mother I'm sorry about your gown, and I'll be happy to compensate her if you're unable to get it clean." He swept her into his arms as she'd requested and headed back toward the yard where her buggy was tethered.

A contented sigh escaped her as her arms wrapped about his neck. "Oh, Titus. You're such a gentleman. I was a fool to turn you down. And that's what I came to tell you."

They were reaching the clearing, and all he wanted was to put her down on the firmer ground so that no one would see him carrying Prissy.

"Are you listening, Titus?" Her emotion-filled words were spoken softly against his ear.

Waves of dread washed over him, and a knot lodged in his throat at her next words.

"I have reconsidered your offer, my darling. I will marry you, after all."

He stopped dead in his tracks and turned his head to look at her. The movement brought them face-to-face—much too close for retreat. Obviously mistaking his action as an invitation, Prissy closed her eyes and pressed her lips to his before he could make a move.

He pulled quickly away and set her down.

"Prissy. . ."

"Oh, Titus. Our first kiss." She wrapped her arms through one of his. "Was it all you'd hoped it would be?"

More than he'd bargained for was more like it. As he walked her to the wagon, he tried to formulate the words to let her down gently.

"Prissy, listen to me." He disentangled himself from her solid grip. She was quite strong for a woman.

"Yes, my darling?"

"I'm not still. . .I mean. You honor me with your decision. But. . ."

"Oh, Titus." She patted his cheek. "You are just too sweet. Please come by tonight and speak with my father, all right? Then mother and I can begin planning the wedding."

Without giving him another chance to speak, she held out her hand. Dumbfounded, Titus took her hand and assisted her into the buggy.

"Don't forget, now. Come to dinner tonight. Six o'clock."

Not sure what had just happened, he stumbled into the house.

Bryce whistled. "Guess Prissy changed her mind."

Titus jerked his head up. "Huh?"

"We watched the whole thing from the window."

Panic exploded inside of him. Titus searched the room until he found Alisa at the counter washing dishes. She kept her gaze focused on the dishpan. Ignoring the rest of the family, he strode across the room and cupped her elbow, turning her to face him. "It wasn't what it looked like."

Her gaze settled on his lips, and she arched an eyebrow. Taking the dish towel from the counter, she handed it to him and walked toward the bedroom. Frowning, Titus watched her leave. He turned a questioning glance on Miriam.

Her lips were tight. "You have Prissy's lip stain smeared all over your mouth." She shook her head. "I don't know how you're going to fix this one. But Alisa is worth ten of Prissy."

Bryce tossed his napkin on the table and leaned his chair back on two legs. "If Titus is going to marry Prissy. Does that mean Alisa's fair game?"

Gideon's booted foot shot out, knocking Bryce off balance. Chair and all, he landed with a thud on the floor.

"Hey! I just meant Titus don't need two women. I want one of them."

Miriam patted Titus's shoulder. "You have a decision to make. You'd best make it fast before you lose Alisa. Bryce isn't the only man around here who's going to be coming around wanting to court her. She'll have ten proposals before the week's out."

Alarm shot through Titus. She was right. He had to get out of this predicament with Prissy. The sooner the better.

eight

Loose strands of hair flew up, tickling Alisa's cheek as she lifted the quilt and let it settle back to the bed. True to his promise, Titus had removed his things from the cabin just before mounting a horse and riding toward town.

Miriam had provided her with fresh bedding and instructed her to take as much time as she needed to make this little cabin her own. The thought of being all alone sent an ache of loneliness through Alisa. She'd never been alone before. It had been difficult enough to grow accustomed to sleeping in a vast house with only Mrs. Worthington, Robert, and Marietta. She wondered if she would ever fall asleep without the sounds of children snoring, the sounds of the city moving about outside her window. The Chance family bewildered her. They were a close-knit bunch, given to arguing at the drop of a hat and just as quick to defend one another.

Throughout the afternoon, one by one she'd had a visit from each brother with the exception of Daniel. And of course, Titus. Each assured her that Titus thought he liked Prissy until he met Alisa. Though she appreciated their thoughtfulness, she'd felt compelled to remind each in turn that she'd only just met Titus. She certainly had no hold on him, and furthermore, she wasn't looking for a husband.

But whether she was looking for a husband or not, it was difficult to push aside the memory of Prissy White in Titus's arms and the sight of that kiss. He'd tried to explain that he was an innocent recipient of the kiss and that he was relieved Prissy had turned down his proposal and he had no intention of going through with a wedding.

But if that was the complete truth, then why had he headed toward town with the instructions not to hold supper for him? She felt safe in assuming he would be eating with Prissy and her parents. And newly acquainted, notwithstanding, the thought didn't sit well with her. So she poured her energy into cleaning her new home.

Titus wasn't the most meticulous housekeeper. The multi-colored rag rugs were in desperate need of washing. The wooden planks, too, needed a good scrubbing. She opened the window to let in a bit of chilly autumn breeze in order to freshen the air inside the room. Her favorite discovery was a wooden slab that folded down and became a desk.

At lunchtime, Miriam knocked on her door. She looked about and nodded appreciatively. "This room hasn't sparkled so much since I lived here."

Alisa laughed. "I believe it."

"The Chance men have their good qualities, but neatness isn't among them. I suppose that's why God sent us."

Alisa glanced down, embarrassed.

"May I give you a bit of advice?"

"Of course."

"Don't discount Titus because of this misunderstanding."

"I don't know what you mean. I can't discount someone I never counted in the first place. Titus is a nice man. So is Paul and. . ."

A frown creased Miriam's brow. "Do you fancy Paul? I just assumed Titus was the one."

"Well, no. I mean I don't fancy Paul. I don't even know

him." Alisa dropped to the bed and looked up at Miriam. "My point is that Titus is free to marry Prissy or anyone else he chooses. I don't have any hold on him any more than I do on Paul or Bryce or Daniel."

"I see." She cleared her throat. "Well, I came to tell you lunch is just about ready."

"Oh, I should have helped cook."

"Nonsense. Today was your day to settle in. Tomorrow we'll get you acquainted with the ranch and discuss what chores you can take over."

Miriam's warm smile eased Alisa's tension. She nodded. "All right. I'll wash the dirt off my hands and be right over."

❧

Paul had just said the prayer when the rattle of a wagon outside drew attention away from the venison stew.

"Looks like word's gotten out already."

Daniel grunted. "That's all we need. To feed half the men in town again."

Miriam's laughter filled the room. "When I first came to the ranch, the men of Reliable took to dropping by at mealtimes. Often up to ten at a time."

"Until I put a stop to it," Gideon said, taking his wife's hand. He gave it a squeeze and stood.

"It's Marv Wall."

"Titus ain't going to like this," Logan said around a bite of bread.

"Titus has his own mess to clean up right now," Daniel grumped. "Serves him right."

Alisa could feel herself slinking further into her chair, wishing she could just disappear altogether from this meal and this conversation. It was too late to slip out the door and to her cabin, as Gideon had already invited the man in. Alisa tried not to look away, but the man's steady gaze and wide eyes made her uncomfortable.

"I heered ya got another one," he said, remembering to slip his beat-up, greasy hat from his head. Sweat stained his armpits all the way down his sides. A grizzled beard stubbled his face. Alisa thought she might be ill.

"Good afternoon, Mr. Wall," Miriam spoke up. "Would you like to join us for lunch? We just finished saying grace."

His face lit up. "Don't mind if I do, Mrs. Chance."

Alisa had never been more aware of anything as she was of the empty seat beside her. Apparently that suited Mr. Wall, for he nearly leaped toward the seat. Miriam took his arm and steered him to the other end of the table.

"Fine. Why don't you take Logan's seat? It's really the best seat at the table."

"Oh, but I was just going to—"

"Nonsense, Logan doesn't mind scooting over." A sweet smile curved Miriam's lips, and Alisa wanted to hug her. "After all, you are a guest."

Logan grinned at Alisa and winked. She couldn't help but return the scamp's smile as he scooted next to her. Suddenly her heart grew light. Thanks to God's intervention, she had landed smack in the middle of a large, loving family who seemed bent on helping her. And Titus or no Titus, she felt as though she belonged.

&

Titus swallowed hard and tried again, wishing desperately White's wasn't the only store in town. "I need enough material for two dresses for Miss Worthington."

Prissy's scowl only deepened. "Why should you be buying

clothes for your servant?"

"First of all, she isn't a servant. And second, she needs clothing and a warm coat. As long as she's living under our roof, we're responsible to see that she has everything she needs."

"I should think you'd care more about your fiancée's feelings than about your hired help."

"Well, about that. . ."

Her smile could have lit up the room. Titus swallowed hard. How had he gotten himself into such a mess?

"Prissy, I came to tell you that I—"

"Hi there, Titus." Reba White entered from the back room. "Nice to see you. Is this business, or couldn't you wait until supper tonight to see my girl?"

Prissy giggled. "Mother, you're embarrassing me."

Sure she was.

"To tell you the truth, we've hired a young woman to help Miriam around the ranch."

"Now, why would you go and do a thing like that when you'll be adding my Priscilla to the ranch soon?" Reba waved toward Prissy. "She'll be plenty of help."

"Now, Mother, I'm not much good at cooking and cleaning. You know that."

"Sure, but once you marry, you'll need to take care of your man. We discussed this. Remember?"

"Yes, but with Miriam doing the cooking—"

"You'll have to learn, just like every other woman does." Reba's voice had taken on a hard edge, and she glanced sharply at Titus. "So this young woman. Is she the one you had supper with last night at the station?"

"Yes, ma'am. She came in on the stage."

"I figured that. What's she needing?"

"As I was telling Priscilla, enough material for two dresses and any other things women need. You'll be a better judge of that than I would. And a coat."

Prissy gave a harrumph and flounced toward the back.

With a shake of her head, Mrs. White jerked her thumb in the direction the girl had gone. "Don't mind her. She'll learn the ropes in no time."

"Yes, ma'am."

Mrs. White peered closer. "You havin' second thoughts, Titus?"

Was he that transparent, or was Mrs. White a mind reader? Whatever the case, it was too bad her daughter wasn't as astute.

"No need to answer. I can see she doesn't take your fancy anymore. Is it the new girl?"

Titus felt his cheeks warm, and he averted his gaze.

"Never mind. I can see it written all over your face."

"I'm sorry, Mrs. White. I tried to tell Priscilla the truth but—"

"Oh, I know. Once she gets something into her head, there ain't no convincing her. I wondered why she'd gotten herself all fired up to go out to the ranch this mornin'." She gave a dismissive wave. "Don't you worry yourself none about it. I'll take care of that daughter of mine. She has a dozen standing proposals. I'm sure one's just as good a catch as another. She won't be upset for long."

Relief flooded Titus from his hairline to his toes.

"Guess you'd best not come to supper, though. Mr. White might not take this as rationally as me."

"Yes, ma'am."

"All right. You come back in an hour, and I'll have your order ready."

Titus thanked her and stepped outside. "Titus, hold up!"

He turned to find Todd Dorsey striding toward him. "What are you doing off the ranch today, Todd?"

"Thought I'd come in and get a haircut and a shave."

The saloon keeper doubled as a barber, and from the nicks on Todd's face, Titus figured the man had been drinking before he took the razor in hand.

"I. . .uh. . .thought I'd come over for a visit this evening. Heard you're breaking a new colt."

"That's right. Bryce's working on it." Titus eyed the man suspiciously. He was no fool. A new colt being broken was no reason to go visiting, especially when the same thing was going on at his own ranch. Alarm bells rang inside of him. He didn't even have to ask the question on the tip of his tongue.

"I hear you're hidin' a real pretty girl at Chance Ranch."

"We're not hiding anyone."

"Then there ain't a girl out there?"

"I didn't say that."

Todd's eyes narrowed. "Then what *are* you sayin'?"

Expelling an impatient breath, Titus shrugged. "Miss Worthington came in on the stage and needed a place to stay. Miriam could use the help, so we offered her a job in exchange for room and board."

Satisfied?

Todd wasn't satisfied. Not by a long shot.

"So no one's got dibs on marrying her yet?"

"Dibs? You make her sound like the last piece of chocolate cake." Titus cringed at his analogy.

Todd grinned. "Well, ain't that sorta like what she is? I'm moseyin' on out there to get my offer in 'fore someone beats me to it."

"Now hold on just one minute." Anger began to rise, and Titus took a steadying breath to control himself. "No one said she wasn't already called for."

Todd frowned. "Ya mean she's already promised to one of ya?"

"Well, no, but I. . ."

"Then she's fair game. You Chances got the last woman, and that was only fair seein' as how she's your brother's wife's sister and all, but it's someone else's turn, and I plan for it to be me."

With that, he mounted his horse and took off at a gallop toward the ranch.

Titus hurried to his horse and mounted quickly. Wishing he still had Raven, he turned the sorrel toward home. His faithful old horse would have gotten him home before Todd could get there. As it was, he knew a couple of shortcuts.

He was halfway home before he remembered the dress goods he'd ordered from Mrs. White. With a groan, he whipped back around. Hopefully Alisa wouldn't take a fancy to Todd or anyone else before he could get back and announce that his wedding was once again off.

nine

Choosing her words carefully, Alisa smiled at Mr. Wall. "Yes, Mr. Wall. I can see how a woman would be blessed to marry a man with a ranch as vast as yours." He'd spent the last few minutes spouting every acre of land, every piece of livestock, and his future plans.

The man's chest swelled. Indeed, his modest acreage, though it couldn't be compared with Chance Ranch, was quite impressive. Of course, a woman would have to look past the excessive sweating, the missing teeth, and the layer of dirt on his neck for him to find someone to share his life with. And she certainly wasn't that woman. Mr. Wall had come for lunch and had stayed for the entire afternoon, despite Miriam's hints that he surely had work that needed attending at his own ranch. He seemed intent upon staying at Alisa's side. They'd been sitting on the bench just outside the door to the main house since lunch.

Alisa was having trouble keeping her eyes open, and the smell was beginning to give her a headache.

The pounding of horse's hooves drew her attention toward the road.

"Well, if that don't just beat all." Mr. Wall's disgust was clear.

"Is something wrong?" Alisa asked.

"There sure is something wrong. I was here first, that's what. Todd Dorsey must have caught wind of you. Now he's coming to try and take you away."

"I beg your pardon?"

"Someone must've been yappin' about you being here at the ranch." He put a protective arm around her shoulders.

Alisa gasped and pulled back sharply. "Please keep your distance, Mr. Wall, or I'll be forced to ask you to leave."

"Sorry, miss," he muttered. "Just don't want there to be no mistakin' who was here first."

The horse pulled to a halt, and a young man dismounted. He removed his hat and grinned, showing a much more promising set of teeth. "Hello. My name's Todd Dorsey. You must be Miss Worthington."

"Why, yes, I am." Alisa found herself responding to his manners.

Miriam appeared on the porch, like an answered prayer.

"Good afternoon, Mr. Dorsey. What brings you all the way out here?"

"You know good and well what brung him," Mr. Wall accused.

Mr. Dorsey gave a sheepish grin. "I saw Titus in town. He mentioned that Miss Worthington here was as pretty as a flower and hadn't been picked yet."

"Hadn't been picked yet!" Alisa squared her shoulders and narrowed her gaze.

"Well, in a manner of speaking. He said you wasn't spoken for."

Alisa's heart sank. Titus was shuffling her off to other men? He must have decided to marry Priscilla White after all.

"Titus was wrong," Mr. Wall declared, stepping forward. "I picked her. I'm claimin' her right now. So you kin just go on and get outta here."

"You can't claim her. I'm claimin' her." The two men stood

nose to nose. Alisa feared they might come to blows.

"Gentlemen, please," Miriam's voice remained low and conciliatory. "Don't you agree that Miss Worthington has the right of choice in the matter of who will be her husband? Marv, you were here first, so you were certainly at an advantage. But Todd rode all the way out here to meet Miss Worthington, so the least you can do is step aside and give him a chance to get to know her as well."

Marv turned to Alisa. "You choose then. Me or him."

Alisa gasped. "I. . .I. . .I don't know what to say."

"Now, gentlemen. Don't be silly. Miss Worthington isn't going to choose one of you right here and now. She doesn't even know you."

"That's right." Alisa's relief that Miriam was here knew no bounds. She only wished she could escape the men who seemed bent on getting her to an altar.

"Now, a real gentleman would realize that Miss Worthington is dead tired from her long trip from San Francisco. I should think a man might show his consideration by letting her rest. That sort of man might make a good impression."

Luckily, Alisa was forced to stifle a weary yawn at just that moment.

Understanding flickered in Todd's eyes. He gave a gallant bow. "Miss Worthington, may I call on you tomorrow evening?"

"Now, wait just a cotton pickin' minute. I was about to ask."

"Why don't you both come to supper tomorrow night?" Miriam suggested. Alisa glanced at the woman. Whose side was she on anyway? Surely she realized Alisa would never be interested in either of these men. Both paled considerably in comparison to Titus. Of course, he'd called her an unpicked flower! Apparently he had no interest in her after all.

The sound of horse's hooves interrupted once more, and with great trepidation, Alisa lifted her gaze toward the sound. "Titus," she breathed.

"Yes," Miriam said, a smile crossing her lips as she nodded. "I guess he'll be home for supper after all.

Unpicked flower.

Suddenly the humiliating situation of having two unsuitable men fighting over her while the one she admired was handing her to them on a first-come, first-served basis was more than she could manage. "Excuse me, please." Turning on her heel, she fled to her cabin. Once inside, she leaned against the closed door and shut her eyes.

Tears slowly pushed past her lashes. She flung herself across her bed. Wave after wave of images rolled over in her mind. Discovering her grandmother only to lose her in a flash. Being implicated by her own father, the despair of running away before the police arrived, wandering all night and all the next day unsure what to do, but knowing she couldn't go back. Nor could she return to the orphanage. After buying a half-rotten apple from a street vendor, Alisa had found the stage station and bought a ticket to take her as far as she could go. Reliable was the end of the trail for her.

Were her only options to marry the likes of the men represented here today? Or should she go back to San Francisco and hope that the police would believe her? But wouldn't they take Robert Worthington's word over hers? After all, he owned a prominent shipping company, and she was merely an orphan working in the Worthington household. Despair filled her and the tears became a river until sobs shook her.

ïê

Titus paced the floor. Alisa had been in that cabin all afternoon, and now she'd failed to show up for supper.

"Titus, please be still. You're making me nervous."

He glanced up in surprise at Miriam's words.

She shoved a filled plate at him. "Why don't you take this to her?"

Relief flooded him. "Good idea."

Letting the door slam shut behind him, Titus headed for Alisa's cabin. He frowned. It was completely dark; not even the soft glow of candlelight filtered through the window. He stopped at the front door and knocked.

No answer. He knocked again, harder this time. "Alisa?"

Finally, a muffled sound assured him that she was inside. The lump began to dislodge. He'd been afraid that perhaps she'd left without telling anyone.

The door slowly opened. She stood before him, her hair and clothing disheveled, but she'd lit a candle.

"We were worried when you didn't show up for supper."

The soft flame highlighted her drowsy smile. "I must have fallen asleep."

"I brought you a plate."

Her smile widened. "That was thoughtful of you."

So entranced was he at the vision she made, Titus said the first thing that popped into his mind. "It was Miriam's idea."

Her expression fell. "I see. Well, be sure to thank her for me." She started to close the door. Titus put his hand out to stop it. "I'm not marrying Priscilla."

"Oh, I'm sorry."

"You are?"

"Aren't you?"

"No."

"I see."

She saw a lot but never the full picture as far as Titus could tell. "The fact is, I don't love her."

Staring mutely, she seemed to be waiting for him to expound. Titus was at a loss for words, but he wanted her to be clear that he intended to court her. "I know it's awkward. And we haven't known each other long, but I'd like to. . ."

Her eyes widened.

"Do you think you'd be willing to allow me to court you?"

A light flashed in her eyes. At least he thought it was a light. He couldn't be sure, because whatever it was left almost as fast as it had shown up.

She shook her head. "I'm sorry, Titus. You've been so kind to me, and I truly appreciate all you've done."

Disappointment seeped through him. That didn't sound like she was building up to "Thank you, I'd be honored." She was about to turn him down flat.

"Alisa, I thought there was something between us."

"It's just not possible. I. . .you don't know me."

"Then let me *get* to know you." Stepping forward, he cupped her cheek. "I can see in your eyes that you feel the same thing I do."

She covered his hand for a second then stepped back. "You're mistaken, Titus. I plan to stay only through the winter. That should give me enough time to earn a train ticket east."

"East? What's back East?"

"My future." This time Titus didn't stop her as she closed the door. What could he say? If she didn't want him, there was nothing he could do about it. With a scowl, he strode to the cabin he shared with Paul, pulled three packages from his saddlebags, and carried them back to Alisa's cabin. He knocked on the door.

"Titus, please," she said when she answered. "I thought I made myself clear."

He shoved the packages toward her. "To make you some dresses."

Her lips opened slightly as she took in a sharp breath of air. "For me?"

"Yes. That dress of Miriam's is too short."

"You're right. Thank you, Titus. Please deduct it from my salary."

He opened his mouth to object, then realized the longer it took her to pay off the things she needed, the longer it would take for her to raise railway fare back East.

"All right." With that he spun around and walked away. Including the cost of the coat, that ought to be an extra month that she had to stay. And during that time, he would do everything in his power to convince her not to go.

ten

Robert Worthington had no time or patience for games. During the past two weeks, the posters with Alisa's sketch had brought out every thief and lowlife from the very dregs of society in and around San Francisco. Most demanded more money or else. In every case, it hadn't taken long to realize that none had truly seen her.

He had no reason to believe these two men standing in his office were any different. Hope deferred caused him to eye the two men, disheveled and dirty, with suspicion. He had become adept at pegging the liars within five minutes. So far, he hadn't made a decision about these two.

The one who seemed to be the leader tossed a frayed poster onto Robert's desk. "You lookin' for this gal?"

Alisa's heart-shaped face stared back at him. "That's right. And I'm sure you've seen her." His tone was laced with sarcasm, but the men didn't seem to notice.

"Maybe." Black eyes bore into Robert, making him uncomfortable. "You still offerin' five hundred dollars?"

"Not for information."

"How much for information?" the other man piped up.

"Shut up, Amos. That ain't what we're sellin'."

"What exactly are you selling, then?" Robert's interest piqued. He kept his voice calm. His muscles twitched beneath the woven fabric of his white shirt like a restless horse impatient for a race to begin.

Something flickered in the man's dark eyes, and Robert braced himself for a demand of more money.

"We saw this girl." He jammed his forefinger down on Alisa's image. "Like the poster said, we want five hundred dollars to bring her in."

"Where and when did you see her?"

"About two months ago. She was on a stage about a half-day's ride east of here.

"You sure it was her?"

"Yep."

Robert steepled his fingers atop his desk and scrutinized the pair. "She probably won't come willingly. As a matter of fact, I can guarantee she won't. Are you willing to kidnap her in order to bring her home?"

"Would we be here if we weren't?" His sneer grated on Robert, igniting his ire. This idiotic pair was the first real lead he'd had in the past two months that Alisa was alive and still in California. He didn't want to anger them, so he gulped down the sarcasm and forced a tight smile.

"All right. Then I suggest you get to it."

"Now hang on a minute. We want half of the money up front. By my calculation that's two hundred dollars."

Idiot.

"The poster clearly states the reward for bringing the girl home is five hundred dollars. When she is sitting across from me, you'll get your pay. Not a penny until then."

Those dark eyes narrowed. "Then maybe we'll just mosey on and do somethin' else."

"I thought you said we need this money, Bart," the other man said, the look of confusion in his sunken eyes nothing short of comical.

Bart scowled. "Shut up, Amos."

Robert reached into his pocket and pulled out fifty dollars. He tossed it onto the desk. "This is all you're getting until you bring Alisa home."

With a black-gloved hand, Bart reached forward and snatched up the bills. "All right, you have a deal. But first I want to know something."

"And that is?"

"What's the girl to you?"

From the way the man seemed poised to strike, Robert surmised any information would be used against him. If he said she was his daughter, the reward would become a ransom and most likely double or even triple. If he acted nonchalant, even a couple of fools like these two would assume he was bluffing. So he arched his brow. "That's my business."

"She's quite a looker."

Amos snickered. "Almost stole me a kiss from her."

Darting his gaze to the simpleton, Robert felt the blood leave his face. "What do you mean?"

"She didn't have nothin' to steal, so I was going to steal a kiss."

"Shut up Amos," Bart snarled.

"Well, looks like I'm gettin' a second chance at that kiss," Amos persisted.

Alarm clenched Robert's gut. "You'll keep your filthy hands off her. Do you hear me?"

A sly smile curved Bart's thin lips, revealing missing teeth. "So she means more to you than you're letting on."

Why couldn't he just think of her as a maid who was stealing his inheritance? Robert inwardly kicked himself for being a softhearted fool. "The girl means nothing to me, but I'm telling you not to harm her or I won't pay a dime."

"Or maybe you'll pay anything to have her back no matter what shape she's in."

For the first time in his life, Robert felt real fear for someone else. If he didn't get his bluff in on these two outlaws before they walked out the door, Alisa might be in more danger than he'd bargained for. He didn't want the girl violated or hurt in any other way. And until now he hadn't thought about anything leading up to her return. He might be a desperate man, but he wasn't a monster. The thought of what could happen to her at the hands of immoral bandits sickened him. Leaning forward to make his point, he curled his lips into a deliberate sneer. "Or maybe the marshal would be real interested in knowing who's been robbing stagecoaches and unsuspecting riders between here and Sacramento."

"Hey, Bart. Maybe we better get goin' and forget the gal."

"Shut up, Amos."

Bart pressed forward, leaning his weight on massive hands, and practically came across the desk, closing in on where Robert sat. The outlaw's putrid breath fouled the air between them. "I don't like threats."

Forcing himself to stand on trembling legs, Robert clenched his fists to control his fear. "Neither do I. Do we understand each other?"

The man glared but nodded. "We will bring her back untouched."

"What about the kiss she owes me!"

"Untouched!" Strangely, Bart's growl reassured Robert.

As the two men stalked to the door, Bart called over his shoulder. "We'll be back."

The door slammed shut behind them. Robert's legs refused

to hold him another second, and he sank back into his chair. The paltry sum Mother had left him was about gone. Thankfully, part of her wishes had stated that household expenses be paid automatically through Mr. Chadwick's law firm until Alisa was well versed in household management.

If he didn't find Alisa soon, he'd be destitute. For now, no one could kick him out of the house. At least not until the time came for it to be sold and the proceeds given to charity as Mother had stated in her will. The thought sent a shiver of anger through him, renewing his determination. Alisa would be found, and one way or another she would relinquish control of the inheritance that was rightfully his in the first place.

❧

"Aunt Miri-Em, Ginny Mae's doing it again. Hurry!"

At the sound of Polly's shrill, four-year-old voice, Alisa leapt up from her desk and flung her door open. Miriam had already exited her cabin and had made a beeline for the garden. It didn't take much to guess what the child was up to. She sat in the middle of the harvested garden, her hands caked with black dirt. From chin to nose, her face bore the evidence of her latest venture. The child just couldn't stay away from worms.

Miriam's face blanched. "Ginny Mae, dumpling. Please come out of the dirt." Her thin voice seemed to come from far away, and Alisa grabbed her arm.

"Are you all right? You're as white as a ghost."

Miriam's head moved slightly in a weak nod. "I think I better go lie down. . . . Will you please take care of her?"

"Of course. Do you need some help getting inside?"

Miriam shook her head. "I can make it." She headed toward the house but made a detour and disappeared into the privy.

"Miss Alisa, she's got another one. Stop her!"

Alisa grabbed Ginny Mae just in time to keep her from popping another fat worm into her rosebud mouth.

"Little girl," she said, sweeping her up and out of temptation's way. "Worms are not a proper meal. And I fear you've made your poor auntie Miriam ill."

"Mum?" The little girl's wide eyes were hardly concerned, but they held a world of questions that Alisa had no doubt would begin bursting out as soon as her mind could form enough words.

"Yes, Mum." Alisa tickled the little girl's belly. Ginny giggled, pushing her hand away.

Miriam appeared a moment later, her face void of color, and she clutched her stomach. It didn't take a doctor to figure out that she'd lost her breakfast. "Come on, girls. Let's get your auntie into bed, and then we'll get Miss Ginny Mae all cleaned up."

Obviously too weak to protest, Miriam accepted the assistance, and they got her settled into bed. Next, Alisa lifted the washtub down from the wall. She grabbed two buckets and headed out to the pump. She returned to the cabin, settled Polly at the table with a picture book, and started the water warming on the stove.

The sun was almost directly overhead, so she knew she'd have to move fast to finish up Miriam's lunch preparation for the men, bathe Ginny Mae, and have everything looking presentable by the time Titus and his brothers came in for their noon meal.

While she peeled and sliced potatoes for frying, Alisa kept an eye on Ginny, who sat on the floor playing. Thankfully, the two women had just made bread the day before, so there was plenty of that left. By the time the potatoes were peeled and sizzling in the frying pan, Ginny was splashing in her bathwater, and Alisa was ready to start frying the fish Bryce had left in the sink after his early morning trek to the creek.

The girls were angels, obedient and cooperative, as Alisa moved between tasks in order to accomplish everything in a timely manner. She was just lugging the dirty-water-filled tub outside when the men rode in from the woods.

The sight of Titus dismounting and striding confidently toward her sent a ripple of pleasure up Alisa's spine. There was no denying it. Titus was one good-looking man. Everything about him was appealing, and somehow she couldn't help but wish her life wasn't so topsy-turvy.

"Let me get that for you," he said, taking the tub. "Who had a bath?"

"Ginny Mae."

Daniel scowled. "What's this all about on a Monday afternoon?"

Intimidated as she always became by Daniel's surliness, Alisa cleared her throat. "I'm afraid she got into the dirt. I'm sorry."

"Why wasn't Miriam watching her?"

"She's not feeling well. So perhaps Ginny toddled outside without her knowledge. I was in my cabin writing a letter."

Titus glanced at her sharply, and Alisa cringed, knowing he would ask her whom she was writing to.

Gideon's voice spared her the drill for now. "Miriam's ill?" His face clouded. "Where is she?"

"Lying down."

He tossed Logan his reins and dashed into the house.

"How sick is Miriam?" The concern in Titus's eyes touched

Alisa. What would it be like to have him worrying over her?

She gave him a reassuring smile. "I'm sure she'll be better after she rests awhile. In the meantime, lunch is ready."

"You gave Ginny a bath, looked after Polly, and cooked for all of us?" Admiration shone in his blue eyes, and Alisa drank it in.

She laughed, waving aside his praise. "I learned to take care of a lot of people at the orph—" She stopped and clamped her mouth shut. From the very beginning, she'd determined not to reveal anything about her past. Even a little information might bring disaster on herself and this family. If the law found her and took her back, at least the Chances could honestly say they knew nothing about her.

Unfortunately, Titus wasn't one to let things go. He raised his eyebrow. "The orph? I assume you were going to say orphanage?"

"I'd best get inside and put lunch on the table for your brothers."

"They can get it themselves." Titus took her arm gently. "Tell me about the orphanage. Were you mistreated growing up? Is that why you don't want to talk about it?"

"Oh, no!" The very thought of Mrs. Perryman raising her voice or lifting her hand in anger was ludicrous. A kinder woman never existed. Before Mr. Perryman had passed away, he had on occasion produced the strap but only under strict provocation.

"So you were going to say 'orphanage.'"

"Yes."

"Won't you finally tell me about yourself?" He let his hand slide down her forearm until his fingers tickled her palm just before they laced with hers. "I want to know everything.

Sometimes I think I'm going to go crazy if you don't open up and give me some clue into who you are."

The warmth of his hand sent waves of longing through her. How she would love to tell him about growing up without a real family and how she'd prayed every day and every night for someone to claim her. And how when she finally learned she wasn't alone, her grandmother had died. She longed to tell him that she was wanted for murder, but that she wouldn't, couldn't hurt anyone, let alone the wonderful woman who had given her a name.

"Alisa." Titus pulled her to him, releasing her hand as he snagged her about the waist. "I don't have any intention of letting you go. Not now. Not ever."

"Titus, please," she whispered, though she could barely hear her own voice through the pounding in her ears. "You don't understand."

"Then make me understand. You've been here for two months, and all I've learned about you is your name. Now I know you're an orphan. Did you think that would matter? Is that why you've been so evasive?"

Alisa wanted to laugh, a short, bitter laugh devoid of humor. He didn't even know that much because she wasn't an orphan after all. But she couldn't tell him that. Instead, she shook her head.

"Then what is it? Why can't you trust me? Don't you know how much I care for you?" The pleading in his tone nearly undid her resolve. If he only knew how much she truly cared, he would understand why she couldn't risk making him an accessory to her perceived crime.

"I can't. I wish I could. But I can't."

His face clouded with disappointment, and he released her.

"All right. Have it your way. But I'm still not letting you go."
He stomped away toward the barn.

"Aren't you going to eat lunch?" she called after him.

"I'm not hungry. Let Logan and Bryce fight over my share."

Defeated, Alisa trudged to the cabin. She knew how he felt; her own appetite had fled as well.

She entered the house amid shouts of laughter. Her brow rose in surprise to find Miriam out of bed. Her face, though still peaked, shone with joy. Gideon's chest puffed, and he was grinning as Paul, Logan, and Bryce pounded him on the back.

"What's going on?" Alisa asked, her lips twitching at the merriment.

"Oh, Alisa." Miriam stepped forward and took her hand. "I'm so happy you've come to be with us. I'll be needing you more than ever now."

"What is it?" She frowned, searching Miriam's face for the answers. "Are you all right?"

"I will be." A bit of color tinged her cheeks.

Suddenly Alisa gasped. "Miriam! A baby?"

Miriam nodded again. "I've thought so for a while, but I didn't want to believe it. Gideon finally convinced me."

Daniel shot up from his chair and slammed out the door. Gideon scowled after him. "I'm getting tired of his moping."

Placing a gentle hand on her husband's arm, Miriam shook her head. "Have some compassion. Remember, Hannah died shortly after Ginny Mae was born. You can't blame him if memories are tormenting him. Please be kind and just pray for your brother."

Tenderness, or maybe more accurately a look of cherishing, washed over Gideon's face, and he cupped his wife's cheek.

After pressing a soft kiss to her forehead, he nodded. "You're right." His eyes clouded as he peered closer. "You look tired."

"Don't worry about me, Gideon. Everything will be fine."

"I want you to be careful." He glanced up at Alisa with silent appeal.

The sight of the exchange between these two filled her heart with longing. Would she ever be able to share that sort of love without fear of having it ripped away from her? Pushing back the ache, she smiled at him over Miriam's head and nodded her reassurance.

Miriam turned, her eyes shining. "Well, what do you think of my news, Alisa, dear?"

Alisa threw her arms around the other woman's shoulders. "Oh, I'm so happy for you. I can't wait to hold your new son or daughter. Babies are wonderful."

Laughter bubbled from her lips. "They are, aren't they?"

"Now, you mustn't overdo it. I'll take care of all the heavy chores from now on."

Miriam looked from husband to Alisa and back to Gideon. "Oh, you two are conspiring already, aren't you?"

Alisa grinned as Gideon winked at her. "We certainly are, and you may as well get used to it until the baby arrives."

It was only later that Alisa realized she had practically promised to stay as long as Miriam needed her.

eleven

Standing in the foggy barnyard, waiting for Sunday service to begin, Titus gave an inward groan. He should have known Prissy wouldn't give up so easily. Staring into her tear-filled eyes brought about a myriad of emotions to his chest—none of which was love or desire. Pity maybe. Irritation, a little bit of guilt for his changing affection? What was it about a woman that if a man lost interest, suddenly she wanted him more than air?

Those were her words. "I can't breathe for wanting you, Titus."

"Prissy." *Please give me the words to end this once and for all.* "You were the one who turned down *my* proposal, remember?"

"I know," she whimpered. "But I was so wrong. I see that now. Won't you give me another chance?"

A second chance. That's what he felt like he'd been given. A second chance with the right woman. He shuddered to think where he'd have ended up if Prissy hadn't rejected his proposal in the first place. Stuck is where. Up a creek without a paddle. In a sinking boat. In a pasture with a riled bull. On a bucking horse with a broken saddle strap. Not one scenario he could imagine made him a happily married man. Not even one.

Maybe a man with stronger character would take one look at her ashen face and give in seeing as how he *had* proposed, but Titus couldn't bring himself to consider it. He couldn't bear the thought. Besides, what woman would want a man who was in love with someone else?

Before he thought better of the question, he heard his own voice. "Prissy, I'm in love with someone else. Would you really have me marry you just to keep my word?"

As soon as the stupid words left his mouth, he knew he'd made a big mistake. Her eyes narrowed, nostrils flared, and for a second, that bull-in-the-pasture scenario was looking a bit less dangerous.

Amazing how fast tears dried when fanned by red-hot anger. "Titus Chance, you are a liar and a cad, and I never want to lay eyes on you again. If you prefer that silly, dowdy-looking servant girl to me, then I suspect more is going on out here than meets the eye."

Instinctively, Titus reached out to snag her arm. He'd never been tempted to hit a woman before, and he wasn't seriously tempted now, but if she spread one word of lying gossip about Alisa. . .

"Turn me loose!" She tried to jerk free, but Titus held her fast.

"Not until we get something straight."

Her lips trembled, and he loosened his grip.

"There isn't one improper thing going on at this ranch. Alisa Worthington is a morally upright, Christian woman, and I'll not have her name smeared by a jealous female. Is that clear?"

Again, wrong thing to say. Horrified rage flashed in her eyes. Titus inwardly kicked himself. What kind of an idiot was he?

"Jealous?" she sputtered. "You take my love for you and throw it in my face and then have the audacity to call me jealous?" This time when she jerked away, he released her.

"Of course I didn't mean you were jealous, exactly."

But it was too late. Her hand was poised to strike, and before he could grab her wrist, her palm made contact with his cheek so hard his ears rang. She was beyond reasoning with. "I could have any single man in Reliable, and I chose you, fool that I was. But never fear, Titus Chance. I will not bother you or the woman you love ever again."

She whipped around and flounced quickly toward the barn where benches had been set up in the makeshift church for their Sunday meeting.

During the warm months, they simply stayed outdoors and worshiped together under God's blue sky. There was something awe-inspiring about being surrounded by nature while seeking God. But when the weather turned cold or rainy, the barn was second best. And their neighbors looked forward to the Sunday meetings. The men took turns sharing scripture, and they always sang hymns to the strumming of the guitar.

"You having troubles?"

Titus turned to find the circuit preacher standing next to him. The parson motioned in the direction Prissy had stomped. The skinny fellow stood a head shorter than Titus. His black suit was just a bit crumpled, and his wide-brimmed black hat seemed a little too large for his head. But he had the kindest, sincerest eyes Titus had ever looked into. Heaving a sigh, he nodded. "I asked her to marry me, and she turned me down."

"I'm sorry. But God allows things to happen for a reason. I'm sure He has another woman for you."

"Oh, I know. That's the problem."

The preacher's brow lifted. "How's that?"

"I'm in love with a different woman."

"I'm sorry. I don't understand. Perhaps it isn't my place to inquire, but why did you ask one woman to marry you if you care for another?"

It seemed almost too much trouble to go over it again. But Titus needed to talk to someone, and in the absence of a regular preacher, he had to take counsel when he could get it. So he spilled out the entire story, beginning with his proposal to Prissy and ending with the slap that still smarted.

The preacher's expression remained impressively passive throughout Titus's discourse. When Titus finished, Parson Abe nodded his understanding of the situation. "So the woman you don't love anymore has changed her mind and is begging you to allow her to reconsider, but the one you now want to marry won't even consider accepting you?"

Giving a curt nod, Titus rested his forearms on the corral fence and released a frustrated sigh. "I reckon that pretty much sums it up."

"Sounds like we have some praying to do."

That was it? Where were the words of wisdom? The comfort? Encouragement? Where was the reassurance that God had surely brought Alisa into his life and that it was only a matter of time before she saw the truth and ran into his arms?

He couldn't restrain a scowl. The preacher gave a short laugh. "You were looking for a different answer?"

"I'd hoped."

"Sometimes the answer is easy and obvious. Other times, particularly when other people are involved, we have to pray and trust God to answer in His time, knowing He might just say no."

As much as Titus hated the thought, he knew in his heart the preacher's words held a large measure of truth. He couldn't force Alisa to come to him, and God wouldn't force her. He still didn't know anything about her past, what had brought her to Reliable. Why had she been running away from San Francisco? Whatever the reason, he knew it wouldn't change his feelings for her.

The barn door opened, and Gideon motioned for them to come on.

"Well," Parson Abe said, "I guess it's time to start the service. You folks got any music?"

Titus nodded. "I play guitar and lead a few hymns."

A broad smile lit the round, red-cheeked face. "Wonderful. Do you know 'Amazing Grace'?"

"Yep."

"Good. You planning to sing that one today? I'm kinda partial to it."

"You got it, Parson."

❧

Alisa closed her eyes and listened to the gentle strumming of Titus's guitar. One thing she loved about Titus was that he always seemed to be whistling, humming, or singing.

Through many dangers, toils, and snares,
I have already come;
'Tis grace hath brought me safe thus far,
And grace will lead me home.

His rich baritone rose above the rest of the men's voices. Alisa's heart lurched as he sang. She'd come through danger, toils, and snares. Tears burned her eyes beneath closed lids. The thought of home seemed so unlikely. She had never had a real home. Mrs. Perryman had done her best, but everyone knew that by the time they were eighteen years old, they had to leave and make their own way in the world.

They were blessed. All of the children at the Perrymans' home. Most children in their circumstances were on their own much younger, but Mrs. Perryman felt a child needed to be taken care of years longer. Many did leave by the time they were fifteen or sixteen, but most stayed as long as they were allowed. Alisa had stayed a bit longer because she helped so much with the little ones. God's mercy had stepped in just in time, and Mrs. Worthington had offered her the job as companion.

If only her grandmother had lived, Alisa would have a home. Living at the ranch the last couple of months had made her feel like part of a family for the first time ever. Against her better judgment, she allowed herself a moment to dream. She dreamed of Titus. Of staying here at Chance Ranch. Marrying Titus. Giving him a half-dozen babies. Really being part of a large, wonderful family.

"Let's begin with a word of prayer."

Alisa's eyes flew open as she realized the music had ceased and the parson was now standing at the front of the barn. Her gaze shifted to Titus. Rather than having his head bowed with the rest of the group, he returned her stare. Her face flushed hot. The concern in his eyes made her feel as though he had read her thoughts.

But how could he know that she longed to call the ranch her home? Longed to return his attention? She had done all she could to keep her distance, though she had to admit to herself that it was becoming more difficult. Deep inside, she knew it would probably be best for her to leave, but how could she go now when Miriam needed her? Poor Miriam was sick morning and night. Halfway through the service, she left the barn, looking peaked.

The parson preached a beautifully poignant message about walking in the will of God. Alisa accepted it as God speaking directly to her, commissioning her to stay at the ranch to help Miriam until she could manage on her own. Tears ran freely down Alisa's cheeks as Logan and Bryce, too, seemed to be listening to the call of God. Both boys slipped from their seats and knelt before a makeshift altar while the parson prayed for them.

By the time service was dismissed, the pig slow-roasting over the barbeque pit was beckoning with its smoky aroma. Alisa headed for the main cabin to check on Miriam and set the pies out.

Gideon had beat her to it and sat next to his wife on the bed.

"How is she?" Alisa asked.

Miriam moaned. "The barbeque smell is making me so ill I can scarcely stand to breathe."

"Oh, I'm so sorry. Can I bring you anything to help?"

She shook her head as though the effort to speak was suddenly too great.

Gideon seemed to forget Alisa's presence as Miriam rolled to her side, curled into a ball. He rubbed her back, crooning words of love and reassurance.

Feeling like an intruder, Alisa turned away and nearly collided with Titus. She gasped, stopping short. He reached out to steady her, the warmth of his hands steaming through her sleeves. She could feel the heat from his body, smell the smoke from the barbeque pit on his clothes.

With him standing this close, Alisa had trouble concentrating. Apparently he had the same trouble, for he stared mutely down, his face a profusion of emotion. Everything within Alisa screamed for her to pull away, to run outside to the safety found in the numbers of people cloistered in the barn and beginning to make their way into the yard. As she began a retreat, Titus drew her close until she was forced to stand on her tiptoes. "Stop running from me," he said, his voice close to a growl. "You're driving me crazy."

"Titus," she whispered. "I don't mean to run. . . ." She couldn't finish. Instead, she stared into his blue eyes, becoming lost in the sea of emotion as they silently locked gazes. Only when her lungs began to burn did she realize she'd been holding her breath. Her lips parted slightly to allow an intake of air. Titus's gaze flickered to her mouth, and Alisa knew in a heartbeat what was about to happen. Her stomach trembled as his head dipped closer.

"Well! Nothing is going on, is there?"

Titus released her in an instant and spun around at the sound of Priscilla's indignant voice.

"No wonder you changed your mind about me. Why marry a decent girl when you can have an indecent one at your disposal?"

Alisa gasped, and the world began to spin as she noticed several neighbors, including Reba White, Prissy's mother, standing nearby, listening to the girl's lies.

This was the last straw. From far away, Alisa heard Titus call her name just before her world went black.

twelve

A cool cloth swept across Alisa's wrists and neck. She shifted, trying to move away from the wetness, but it followed her. She moaned.

"That's it, girl, open your eyes."

Frowning, she obeyed. Mrs. White's face hovered above her.

"What happened?"

"You fainted dead away. Titus brought you home, but considering Prissy's big mouth, I thought it best if he not be in here alone with you."

Clarity came rushing back, bringing with it the humiliation she'd felt at Prissy's outburst. "Oh, my."

"Now, don't you worry. I know these Chances. They're decent folks." She went on without waiting for Alisa to comment. "Everyone around here knows Titus is a God-fearing man, and he'd marry you before he got close enough to compromise you. So don't you go thinking anyone believes there's anything improper going on out here."

"Th. . .thank you, Mrs. White." Alisa studied her hands, embarrassed by the entire topic.

"By the way, when will you and Titus be tying the knot?"

"I beg your pardon?"

"Getting hitched? My Prissy says Titus won't marry her because he's in love with you."

A flame of joy flared inside Alisa at the honor of a man like Titus Chance being in love with her, but the truth of the matter came behind like a cold, soaking rain and quickly quenched the flicker of happiness. "Oh, that's not true. I don't know why he isn't marrying Prissy—except she did refuse him first."

A pained look crossed Mrs. White's face. "I know. That girl can't seem to make up her mind. I told her she was being mighty foolish for turning down a Chance man. But she wouldn't listen. Now she decides she wants him after all, and it's too late." She peered closer. "When did you say you two are getting married?"

"We're not." Alisa averted her gaze to the quilt.

Mrs. White's work-roughened hand covered hers. "Unless I miss my guess, that decision is yours, not Titus's." The bed shifted with her weight as she turned slightly. "Do you want to talk about it?"

Alisa bit her trembling lips but shook her head. "I can't."

Somehow, Alisa found herself enveloped in comforting arms, crying out her hurt and disappointment. When her tears were finally spent, Alisa took the handkerchief Mrs. White pressed into her hand. She wiped the wet, salty trails from her cheeks and blew her nose. "Thank you, ma'am."

The older woman took hold of Alisa's shoulders. The look she gave her could only be described as motherly, and Alisa bit her trembling lip to keep from sobbing all over again. "Now listen, honey," Mrs. White said. "I know things can look pretty desperate out here. It's a man's world. That's for sure. But if you're thinking of leaving because of the difficulties, I urge you to reconsider. Take Miriam for instance. She came out here and took over her sister's children, took on six brothers and their messiness and big appetites. Even in the family way and feeling sickly, she glows like a candle.

Happiness is finding where you belong."

"What if you don't belong anywhere?" The question left her before Alisa could rein it in.

Understanding flickered across Mrs. White's features. Her chin jutted upward in a short nod. "I see. You've been dealt a bad hand, and you're running from something."

With no strength to deny it, Alisa merely sighed. "I can't stay here indefinitely and build a life with Titus when my past may bear down upon us one day."

"Maybe you should come clean with him. Give him the choice to decide if it's worth the risk or not."

Alisa shook her head. "He can't know anything about how I ended up here."

"Honey, gal, I can see the weight of the world is nearly more than your skinny shoulders can bear. If you don't tell someone soon, you're going to crack beneath the load. Now, anything you tell me is going to stay right here in this room and in the throne room of God."

How good it would feel to tell someone her troubles. Alisa's heart began to pound against her chest. "You promise you won't say a word? Because if the Chance family knew, it could cause them harm if I was ever found."

A deep frown created twin ruts between Mrs. White's eyes. "You have my word."

Even before she began to speak, Alisa felt the burden lifting. Just knowing she could trust her plight to another human being made her feel a thousand times better. When Alisa finished up with Titus bringing her to the ranch, Mrs. White gave her a tender smile.

"So you see. Titus would move heaven and earth, even at the risk of crossing all five of his brothers, to help someone in obvious need. I think you should open up to him. Tell him the truth. If his feelings for you run as deep as yours do for him, I think he has a right to know."

"My. . .feelings?"

"Every time you say his name, your face softens. You care for him. And I can't say that I blame you. Now, I believe every word of your story, and Titus will as well. He's saved you once, and unless I miss my guess—and I rarely do—he'll do whatever it takes to prove your innocence."

"But it doesn't seem fair that he should be placed in that position. Wouldn't it be better if I left and gave him the chance to turn to another woman? Prissy, for instance, cares for him a great deal." The very thought of Titus ending up with that hussy left a bitter taste in Alisa's mouth. But perhaps if he were to fall back in love with the other girl, Alisa's leaving, once Miriam was back on her feet, wouldn't be as hard for him to swallow.

Mrs. White expelled a short laugh. "Once a man like Titus Chance finds real love, he won't settle for anything less." She stood. "Honey, I understand why you don't want to open up to Titus, and I admire your reasons, but if you leave, I have a feeling he'll come after you. Men like him don't come along very often, and when they do, they don't give up very easily."

The thought of Titus coming after her sent a tremor through Alisa's stomach. Memory of being held in his arms just before Prissy burst in on them made her heart slam against her chest.

He'd almost kissed her. There had been no question that she would have allowed it to happen. Not only allowed it, but she most likely would have kissed him back. Weakness spread over her. If she was going to stay at the ranch for a few more months, she could never, ever let that almost happen again. No matter how she might long to feel his arms around her. Feel his kisses.

"I'll leave you to gather yourself together." Mrs. White stood.

"Oh, but I should get up and put the food out on the tables."

Mrs. White patted Alisa's shoulder. "I'll take care of that. You can come out and help when you're ready."

Alisa lay back on the bed and stared at the ceiling.

Through many dangers, toils, and snares,
I have already come;
'Tis grace hath brought me safe thus far,
And grace will lead me home.

Tears trickled down the side of her head and dampened her pillow.

❧

Hiding behind a large oak tree in front of Mrs. Perryman's orphanage, Robert Worthington felt like a peeping Tom. And he hated that feeling. But after two weeks, he'd still heard nothing from those two outlaws, Amos and Bart. Rage burned inside of him at the very real possibility that they'd taken the fifty dollars he'd paid up front and forgotten all about Alisa and the five hundred dollar reward.

With a self-deprecating chuckle, he continued to watch the house. Why should he be surprised that a pair of thieves stole? But that left him to form another plan of action. And that plan just walked outside.

A boy who appeared to be in his late teens trotted down the steps, leaving the door to bang shut behind him.

"Jonesy, really!"

"Sorry, Mrs. Perryman."

Robert knew the boy would be headed toward the ice warehouse where he would work loading blocks of ice into the ice wagons all night. He'd been watching him. The kid worked hard. He had to hand it to him. Maybe too hard for the measly salary he was sure the boy earned. Robert had a hunch Jonesy might be leaving the orphanage soon and would be looking for a way to make more money.

Able to draw funds from the shipping company, Robert had formed the idea. He stepped out just as Jonesy reached the tree.

"Yeow!" The lad jumped back and assumed an attack stance.

"Settle down," Robert said, holding up his hands.

"What are you doing sneaking around in the middle of the night?" Jonesy asked.

"I could ask you the same thing." No sense letting the boy know he'd been watching him. That would definitely put him on the defensive.

"Going to work, not that it's any of your business." He turned and resumed his gait.

Robert followed and quickly caught up to him, easily matching him stride for stride. "Where do you work?"

"At the icehouse."

"Sounds cold."

A shrug lifted his shoulders. "I guess."

"How would you like to earn a month's pay just for a little bit of information?"

The kid gave a mocking laugh. "And end up with my neck in a rope? Forget it."

"Now, this isn't something that'll get you into trouble. I

just need someone I can count on not to double-cross me. That's all."

"What makes you think you can trust me?"

"I have a gut feeling."

"What would I have to do?"

Robert bit back his grin. Now that he had the kid's attention, it was only a matter of time before Alisa was back at the house. And she would turn her inheritance over to him. . .one way or another.

He placed a fatherly arm around Jonesy's shoulders and smiled. "Tell me, son. Who collects the mail for the orphanage?"

❧

Foggy mist chilled the December air as Titus helped Alisa from the wagon and walked her through the muddy street to the boardwalk in front of the mercantile. He stopped short of escorting her inside. "All right. I'm going over to the feed store. You stay put until I get back to take you home. You hear? This town isn't safe for a woman alone."

As if to punctuate his words, two shots sounded from the end of the street. Alisa gasped. Titus glanced in the direction of the gunfire, then turned back to her, giving her hand a comforting squeeze. "Looks like just a couple of cowboys making their presence known. Nothing to worry about. I'll wait for you to get inside before I head to the feed store."

A smile curved Alisa's lips, and she nodded. "Thank you for your thoughtfulness."

"I'm not being thoughtful." His blue eyes sizzled with emotion as he looked down at her, his hand still clutching hers. "I'm doing everything I can to make sure the woman I love is safe."

Titus was making a habit of sharing his feelings openly. No one could doubt his sincerity. All the more reason Alisa felt she had to discourage his attentions and remind him often that she would be leaving as soon as Miriam recovered from childbirth. She opened her mouth to once more make the announcement, but Titus stopped her with a well-placed finger to her lips. "I know. Don't say it." He lifted her hand and brushed a soft kiss to her knuckles. "Get inside. I'll be back in less than an hour."

Still reeling from his soft touch, Alisa could only nod. He reached around her and opened the mercantile door. He was so close she could feel his breath warm on her face as he shifted back to allow her entrance.

She stepped inside, and he closed the door after her. Alisa watched through the glass as he sauntered away, each step sure and confident.

A snort behind her alerted her to Mrs. White's presence. "That man has no intention of letting you go."

Sighing, Alisa nodded. "You're right about that, I'm afraid."

"Still being stubborn, are you?" A scowl pinched her face. "I think you ought to just tell the whole truth of it and let Titus decide."

"So you said last week," she replied, distracted as Titus glanced back at the mercantile just before disappearing inside the feed store.

"And so I'm saying again, young lady," Mrs. White snapped. If possible, her frown deepened. "They took you in when you had nowhere else to go, made you part of the family. They deserve your honesty."

"You're more than likely right, and if my being honest didn't have the potential to cause them trouble, I'd have told them everything from the first day. But as it is, I can't do it."

"So what brings you into town on such a dreary day?"

Was it a dreary day? Seated shoulder to shoulder with Titus during the hour-long ride had felt like a sunny day in paradise, despite the drizzle. But of course she couldn't tell that to Mrs. White. The woman knew far too much as it was. Only her promise not to reveal Alisa's past gave her peace. Reaching into her reticule, she pulled out the letter she'd composed and a coin to pay for postage.

"I'd like to mail this."

"San Francisco, eh?"

Alisa nodded. She had no secrets from Mrs. White. "I'm sending Mrs. Perryman a donation for the orphanage. Christmastime is always rather worrisome. She tries to buy a little something for each of the children to open Christmas morning. Whenever possible she buys a ham and sweet potatoes and makes apple pie."

Mrs. White's face softened. "I'm sending a donation as well. Those children are going to have a wonderful Christmas this year."

Alisa watched through quick tears as Mrs. White opened Alisa's envelope and slipped some bills inside. After resealing the envelope, she set it aside. "This will go out in the morning and should get to San Francisco in plenty of time."

Clasping the other woman's hand, Alisa looked into her lined face and smiled. "You have no idea what this will mean to them. Thank you."

Mrs. White smiled in return. "I'm glad to do it. You didn't leave a return address, I see."

"No. It's better if she doesn't know where I am. I assured her that I am safe. And I told her all about what happened to my grandmother so that she never thinks I did anything to harm her."

"Anyone who knows you as well as Mrs. Perryman must will know you aren't capable of harming a soul. But I'm sure she'll be relieved to hear that you are safe."

The bell chimed above the door. Alisa turned, expecting to see Titus standing there.

"Well, looky here, Amos. We don't got to look no farther."

"I told you two weeks ago we shoulda come here in the first place, but you had to take us hither and yon."

"Shut up, Amos."

"What are you talking about?" Mrs. White asked.

"The girl. She's wanted in San Francisco, and we come to fetch her back."

"You the law?" Mrs. White eyed the two.

Hysterical laughter bubbled from Alisa's lips. "The law? These are the two men who robbed the stagecoach the day I arrived."

"Then they can forget taking you anywhere."

Bart took a menacing step forward. "Now you just be a nice old lady and don't cause a fuss, and no one'll get hurt. One way or another, we're taking her with us."

"In a pig's eye."

Before Alisa or either of the two men could react, Mrs. White reached beneath the counter and pulled out a shotgun. Bart stopped dead in his tracks. Fear leaped across his grizzled features. "Now, lady. There ain't no need to get jumpy."

"I'd say there is a reason. We don't much care for thieving snakes around here."

"That's right." Mr. White's deep voice coming from the storeroom made Alisa's knees nearly buckle with relief.

"Listen here." Bart stepped back but encompassed them with a dark glare. "I have five hundred dollars riding on taking that girl back to San Francisco, and I don't aim to leave this town empty-handed."

"I aim for you to leave this town in the marshal's wagon, mister." Mr. White snatched the shotgun from his wife's hands. "Now the two of you toss down those side arms."

"What are we gonna do, Bart? I can't go back to jail."

The bell jangled once more, and Prissy flounced through the door. "Hi, Mama. Mr. Wall just dropped me off. We had a dandy lunch." She stopped, her eyes growing wide in the silence. "Wh. . .what's going on?"

Mrs. White gasped as Amos reached out and put Prissy in front of him. Too swift for anyone to react, he produced a hunting knife and pressed it against the young woman's neck. "Well, now. This appears to be my lucky day." He leveled his dark gaze on Alisa. "I'll be back, my sweet. You can count on that."

thirteen

Titus hummed along to the tune of "Amazing Grace" as he guided the team back toward the mercantile. He looked forward to the long ride home with Alisa. Even toyed with the idea of stopping somewhere along the way and insisting she open up about her past. There was no denying she knew where he stood. Every day he fell more deeply in love with her. Her sweet willingness to help out during Miriam's bouts of illness—though they were becoming fewer and farther between—never failed to send a rush of tenderness through him. Even after a hard day of doing her own chores, she was willing to pitch in and help take care of the girls, cook supper, and clean up—generally do everything Miriam used to do alone. He shook his head. The whole group of brothers, himself included, had been nothing but insensitive knuckleheads.

His heart leapt as he pulled up to the mercantile. Maybe he'd carry Alisa to the wagon. This mud was enough of an excuse that she probably wouldn't protest too much. Just as he hopped down, he heard a scream coming from the alley between the mercantile and the next building over. Alisa?

His heart lodged in his throat, and he took off at a run, drawing the newly acquired Colt that his brothers had graciously agreed he needed to replace. In the alleyway, he saw Prissy struggling against a man. The sight of her false curls brought Titus a flash of relief that it wasn't Alisa until chivalry took over, producing the indignation he needed to trot down the alley, careful not to make noise.

"No!" Prissy's muffled voice shrieked.

"Let her go, Amos, and come on!"

Amos? Rage flared within Titus's chest. The thieving, no good outlaws. What were they doing in Reliable?

"Not before I get my kiss."

"We don't got time for that. Let the girl go. She'll only slow us down."

"I ain't lettin' this one go." He gave up the struggle for a kiss and hauled Prissy toward his horse. *My horse!* Titus moved into full view, his pistol pointed in the direction of the outlaws.

"Let the girl go."

"Titus, help me!"

"See what you done, Amos? Get yerself outta this." Bart slapped his horse and took off at a gallop, leaving Amos behind. Keeping his gun fixed on the outlaw, Titus walked forward. "That's right. Step away from the girl."

"Or maybe I'll just keep her, and you can either shoot her or let me go."

"This is going to end badly for you, Amos. Look, Bart didn't even stick around to back you up."

He sneered. "Bart did exactly what I'd have done. A man's gotta look out for hisself."

So much for honor among thieves.

"Titus, do something!"

With a grin, Amos shoved her forward so that Titus had no choice but to catch her or let her fall. She filled his arms, and he watched helplessly as Amos dashed to Raven and rode away after Bart. Regret filled him. If he could've kept Amos, he'd have sent a thief to jail and would have gotten his horse back.

"Oh, Titus. Thank you." Prissy's shivering body brought

him back to the present. She looked up at him with tears flooding her green eyes, and his heart softened. He snuggled her close and allowed her to cry. "Th. . .that horrible man tried to kiss me."

"I know, but he didn't succeed," he soothed.

"B–but, Titus. He said I l–looked like I wanted to be kissed."

Her eyes were filled with question. And that filled Titus with indecision. Should he be honest and tell her that when a woman wore rouge and painted her lips, it gave a man certain ideas about her willingness to be kissed?

Just as he dismissed the idea, she asked him flat out. "Was he right, Titus? Do I look like I want to be kissed?"

Caught between the temptation to lie and spare her feelings or tell her the truth so maybe she would take measures to correct her actions, he hesitated.

"You can tell me the truth," she urged.

"Well, Prissy, you do sort of. Still that doesn't mean a man has any call to go stealing a kiss, but—"

"Are you saying I look like I want to be kissed?"

Swallowing hard, he nodded.

She closed her eyes and pressed closer, rising on her tiptoes. "Then kiss me, Titus. I want to be kissed by you." Before he could shift back in alarm, she pressed his head down until their lips touched. He took hold of her arms and held her away from him.

Triumph gleamed in her eyes. "I know you must care for me, Titus. You're my hero. You came after me."

"When I heard you scream, I thought you were Alisa. I care for her." Anger over her kiss caused the words to come out more sharply than he would have allowed under normal circumstances. "Please, Prissy. I don't want to hurt you, but will you please get it through your head once and for all that I plan to marry Alisa?"

Her eyes narrowed dangerously. "I wish they had taken her like they intended all along. And good riddance."

"What do you mean?"

"They wanted your precious Alisa. I came in at the wrong time, and they used me as a hostage to get away."

She swept past him and headed back to the mercantile.

Titus followed her, rubbing his mouth with the back of his hand and hoping there were no traces of Prissy's red lip rouge on his mouth. He had to resist the urge to toss her into the mud. Instead, he opened the door for her. One glance at Alisa's stricken face melted his anger. As Mr. and Mrs. White rushed to their daughter, Titus opened his arms to Alisa. She walked toward him slowly, as though her legs had little strength, and allowed him to enfold her in an embrace. Her soft sigh told him all he needed to know about her feelings for him. She had been waiting for him to return, had been waiting for his arms.

❧

Robert Worthington stared at Jonesy in surprise. Less than two weeks had passed since they'd made their arrangement, and here the boy was already in his office, holding an envelope in his hands.

"Well, give it to me," Robert said.

"Not until you hand over three dollars and twenty-five cents."

Robert reached into his pocket and gave him five. Jonesy's eyes widened.

"Consider the rest a bonus."

"Thank you." Rather than leaving, he stood watching Robert.

"Well? What are you waiting for? Don't you have to go home to supper or something?"

"I'm waiting for you to be finished so I can take the letter to Mrs. Perryman."

Leveling a firm gaze at the boy, Robert fingered the envelope. "I just paid you five dollars for this letter. It's mine now."

The boy frowned. "She's been worried sick about Alisa. If you think I'm going to give her letter away and let her think Alisa is hurt or dead or something like that, you're crazy. I sold you the right to read it. Not keep it." He tossed the five dollars back on the desk. "Forget the deal. Give me back the letter."

"Now, just hold on. I'll read through the letter and perhaps I'll allow you to take it."

"Read it," the kid said through clenched teeth. "Then hand it over."

Without a reply, Robert glanced at the postmark. Reliable. He'd never heard of such a town, but it shouldn't be very hard to locate. He slid his letter opener beneath the seal and quickly scanned the letter:

Dear Mrs. Perryman,

Please forgive the amount of time that has gone by with no word from me. I am fine and staying with a wonderful family on their ranch. I have become a fugitive, unjustly accused of murder, and though I know the stamp on this letter will reveal my whereabouts, I couldn't bear the thought of the holidays going by without wishing you and the children a Merry Christmas.

I know you would never believe me capable of harming anyone, let alone my grandmother. That's right, Mrs. Perryman. Mrs. Worthington revealed to me that she was my grandmother. Unfortunately, she died very suddenly, and I was accused of her death. I did not cause her death, of that I can assure you, but my father has accused me anyway. I suspect this is because my grandmother was set to give me an inheritance. If only she had lived. A relationship with her would have made me the richest woman alive.

I have enclosed some money. It isn't much, but I hope it will give the children a bit of a Christmas. Perhaps you can buy that goose this year. Annie whispered to me just before I left that she secretly longs for a new pair of pink ribbons like the ones her mother wore the night she died. Do you remember the white dress I always longed for because the mother in my dreams always wore white? I can't help but hope Annie will get her ribbons.

I will try to write again soon.

Kiss the children for me and ask them to pray for me, as I am praying for each one of you.

All my love,
Alisa Worthington

Robert folded the letter, tucked it back into the envelope, and stuffed the bills inside as well. After another cursory glance at the stamp on the front, he tossed the letter back on the desk. "Take it and go."

He averted his gaze to the window until he heard the door open. "Wait just a minute."

"Yes, sir?"

Scowling, Robert pulled his wallet from his coat pocket and

removed some bills. "Give this to Mrs. Perryman," he said. "Tell her to buy the little girl some ribbons and Christmas presents for all of the children. And tell her to buy a goose for Christmas dinner."

Jonesy's face molded into a look of utter disbelief. "What are you trying to do?"

"Nothing. Can't a man give a bunch of orphans a decent Christmas?"

The boy gave him a dubious look. He glanced at the bills in his hand and shrugged. "Whatever your reason, the children deserve a good Christmas. Mrs. Perryman will appreciate this."

Averting his gaze to the desk, Robert gave a dismissive wave. "Close the door behind you."

With a frustrated grunt, he sat back in his chair. The letter held not one clue as to where Alisa might be. It had, however, given him a clue into Alisa. She'd dreamed of her mother wearing white? Robert felt a tremor of guilt then pushed it away with a short laugh. Perhaps her mother would have worn a white dress and married a good man if he hadn't spotted her and lusted after her. Truth was, he couldn't even remember her face. He could, however, remember his daughter's heart-shaped visage. The image haunted him. Reaching into his drawer, he pulled out the sketch of Alisa. What if he'd never taken her away? What if he'd been a father to her as his father had been to him?

He raked his fingers through his hair and laughed at his sentimentality. "You're a fool, Robert Worthington. An utter fool."

❧

Alisa peeked around through the window to make sure the girls weren't inside the main house before she tapped on the door.

"Come in," Miriam called. Her voice sounded strong, and Alisa smiled as she stepped inside. Miriam was just pulling a pie from the oven. The spicy, cinnamony aroma filled the cabin.

"Mmm. Smells heavenly."

"Thank you. It's apple.

"My favorite. You sound like you're feeling better."

"I am! Praise the Lord. I was beginning to think I might be sick for the rest of my life."

Laughter bubbled from Alisa's lips. Even at the orphanage, Christmas had been a time of joy and expectation. This year, despite her situation, her childlike optimism had returned within a week of the ordeal in Reliable, and it continued to permeate these days leading up to Christmas.

"Did you get them finished?" Miriam asked.

"I did."

"You didn't wrap them yet?"

Alisa grinned and shook her head. "I wanted to show them off first."

"Let me put some water on for tea, and I'll be right over."

Miriam wiped her hands on a towel and came over to the table. Alisa pulled out the gifts she'd been working on for the past two weeks in her spare time. She'd had to use Miriam's sewing kit, as she'd left her own back at the Worthingtons' home.

The girls had been such good little helpers that Alisa had made them each an apron. Polly's was made of red gingham, and Ginny Mae's of blue gingham.

"Oh, how darling!" Miriam exclaimed, holding each item close to her heart. Her eyes filled with tears. "I can't wait to begin sewing for the baby."

"It'll be such fun."

Miriam folded the aprons carefully and set them back on the table. She moved to the stove and pulled the teapot from the fire. After pouring two cups, she brought them back to the table then moved back to the kitchen shelves. She fumbled around for a moment then produced some paper and string. "You can use this to wrap them. Their little faces are going to light up when they see those."

"They'll have quite a Christmas. Polly and Ginny Mae are going to adore the dresses you made them."

"Yes. I only wish Hannah were here to see how special those two are."

Alisa covered her hand. "She knows. I'm sure God allows mothers to look down from heaven and see the ones they left behind."

Miriam gave a short laugh. "Then better for Daniel if he never remarries. Because Hannah would never stand for it."

Despite the slight irreverence, Alisa laughed outright. Miriam joined her, and if for no other reason than to relieve the tension of the past few weeks, the two women laughed until tears streamed down their faces. Gideon and Titus entered the cabin to the howling.

"What's this?" Gideon demanded, dropping an armload of wood into the bin.

"We were just talking about Hannah."

"And that made you laugh?" Titus asked.

At the look of bewilderment on the two men's faces, the women laughed even harder.

Still chuckling, Alisa rose. "I best put these under the tree and head back to my cabin."

"I'll walk you," Titus said.

Alisa's pulse quickened. "Thank you, Titus, but it isn't necessary."

"I'd say those two outlaws looking for you make it plenty necessary."

Alisa finished tying the string around the packages and walked to the tree. "Honestly, Titus. It's been more than two weeks since we've seen them. Do you really think they are still hanging around these parts?"

"I don't know. But I'd rather not take any chances."

"I agree with Titus," Miriam said. "No sense risking it."

"Oh, all right." She took her coat from a peg by the door and shrugged into it. They stepped into the chilly night. Titus took her elbow to guide her. She gathered a slow breath of the crisp air. "I love Christmas," she whispered.

"So do I. It seems like it makes the world fresh and new again. Like an innocent baby."

"Like Jesus."

"Yes."

There was no need for them to say more. But Alisa couldn't help but feel the wonder of sharing a love for Jesus with a fellow believer. She didn't understand why her life had taken such a topsy-turvy turn, but God did. And even in the difficult times, He had taken care of her so far. She knew that nothing could separate her from His love. Christmas was a good reminder of that.

As though reading her thoughts, Titus gave her elbow a little squeeze. She smiled at him as they reached the door.

He stepped closer, and for an instant, it seemed as though he might kiss her. Alisa braced herself, unsure whether her heart would lead her head this time or not. A shrill scream tore through the air, taking the decision out of her hands.

She gasped. "That sounded like Polly."

Titus sprinted toward Daniel's cabin, with Alisa close on his heels.

He burst inside. Daniel held his trembling daughter in his arms. Fat tears rolled down Ginny Mae's face as she sat on her bed. Alisa's heart constricted, and she went to the child. She lifted her, cuddling the warm body close.

"What happened?" Titus demanded.

"Polly said she saw someone at the window."

"A man. A big ugly man with a big hat."

A knot thudded in the pit of Alisa's stomach.

Titus stomped to the door and grabbed the lamp from the rail just outside. "I'll be back. Stay put, Alisa."

In a minute, Alisa noticed the lamp's glow from the window. Then he came back. "Daniel, I'd like to talk to you on the porch."

Daniel turned his gaze to Alisa. She nodded. "I'll put them back to bed."

That moment, the rest of the family showed up. "Did I hear a scream?" Logan asked.

"What's wrong? Are the girls all right?" Miriam bustled into the room and looked from one of her nieces to the other. Then to Alisa. The men stayed outside with Daniel and Titus.

"Polly saw someone outside the window."

A flash of concern crossed Miriam's face. "Was she dreaming?"

Alisa shrugged. The door opened. The brothers stomped in. "Here's what we've decided. Alisa's going to bunk with Miriam tonight."

"Good idea," Miriam said.

"Gideon will bed down in the other room instead of going to one of the other cabins."

Miriam smiled at her husband. "We'll feel safer that way."

"And I'm staying, too."

Gideon scowled at him. "I can protect my wife and Alisa."

"Probably." Titus kept his gaze fixed on Alisa so intensely she couldn't breathe. "But I'm not taking any chances."

fourteen

Alisa watched with satisfaction as the stack of pancakes waned. She set another platter on the table amid the oohs, ahhs, and grateful grunts from the brothers. Miriam replenished the platter of bacon and rolled her eyes at Alisa, grinning affectionately as she did so. The holiday seemed to have doubled the men's already healthy appetites. Even Miriam, Alisa noted, nibbled on a bit of bacon and managed to tackle a pancake.

Little Polly seemed to have forgotten the previous night's terror in anticipation of the promise of gifts to be opened directly after breakfast.

Alisa smiled at the two little girls, and her heart ached with longing to see the children at the orphanage. How she wished each one of them could experience this large, loving family. She turned to the tub of dishwater to hide the tears simmering just beneath the surface.

"You didn't eat much." Titus's soft voice next to her ear made her jump. He set his plate down on the counter.

"Gracious, Titus. Don't sneak up on a body."

"Sorry. Why didn't you eat?"

"I did. I'm just too. . ." She was going to say nervous, but one look into his worry-filled eyes convinced her that it wasn't the best thing to say. "Too excited to eat. Christmas is the best day of the year."

"For now."

"For now? What's that supposed to mean?"

He scooped up a finger full of bubbles and brushed her nose. Alisa could feel the bubbles tickling her. She gasped. "I can't believe you did that!"

A chuckle left him. "Your life with me will be filled with little surprises."

Alisa wiped away the bubbles with the back of her hand. "We've already—"

"Shh. Don't spoil it. This is the last Christmas that will be your favorite day. So you'd better enjoy it."

"Titus." She gave him an exasperated look, wiping her hands on the nearest towel. "You aren't making any sense."

He leaned in so close she could feel the warmth of his breath against her cheek. "From now on, your wedding day will be your favorite day of the year. Every anniversary, you'll have a surprise better than the year before."

Alisa wanted to reprimand him. To remind him that she would be leaving in a few months. But she also wanted to wrap her arms around him and beg him to marry her right now. He seemed to understand her conflicting feelings, for he leaned forward and brushed soft, warm lips against her cheek. Then he pressed a box into her palm. "Merry Christmas, Alisa."

"You're supposed to wait until after breakfast, Uncle Titus."

Polly's indignant voice rose up between them.

"You're right, sugar dumplin'," Titus said, swinging the four-year-old into his arms. "But I couldn't wait." He danced her around the room amid giggles and pleas for more. Alisa watched, her mind conjuring the image of Titus holding their own laughing daughters in his arms.

"He'll make a wonderful father, won't he?" Miriam's voice evaporated the fantasy.

Alisa tucked the box into the wide pocket of her apron, determined to return it unopened at the earliest opportunity. "I'm sure he will."

"And a wonderful husband, too. I just love a man who hums and whistles. That's a sign of contentment, which in my opinion is a sign of character."

"Yes, he's definitely going to make some woman a good husband. Titus is a great man. There's none better."

Miriam chuckled. "Well, I could argue with that. But then, I could never convince you. A blessed woman knows there's no one like the man she loves." Her expression grew soft. "Isn't that true?"

Sighing gently, Alisa nodded. "I suppose it is."

"Honey, why don't you give up this notion of leaving us after the baby comes? We all love you and want you to stay. Even if Titus wasn't madly in love, the rest of us adore you."

"Even Daniel?" Alisa laughed at her own joke.

A smile tugged at Miriam's lips. "Well, I'm sure he does in his own way. But let's leave him out of this for now."

"Are you ladies about ready to join us?" Gideon called. "These girls aren't going to be able to restrain themselves from tearing into these packages much longer."

"Just a few more minutes and we'll have everything cleaned up."

"I'll help," Bryce piped in. Not to be outdone, Logan grabbed a stack of plates. Alisa held her breath until they were safely deposited into the water. In no time, amid laughter and teasing, all traces of breakfast were cleaned up and put away.

Alisa's heart soared watching the girls opening their gifts. When Ginny Mae toddled over to her carrying her new little apron, Alisa's heart melted.

"Put on?"

"Of course. Turn around." Alisa wrapped her arms around the child and pressed the apron to the girl's tummy, then tied the strings in back into a large blue-gingham bow. "There. Now you're ready to cook Christmas dinner." Ginny Mae giggled and threw her chubby little arms around Alisa. It was all the thanks she needed. She drank in the sweet baby scent as she rubbed her cheek against the child's silken hair. "You're welcome, precious."

Paper littered the small room a few moments later. The girls, dressed in new outfits Miriam had made and wearing the aprons over them, looked like little princesses. Daniel surveyed his daughters, and Alisa could have sworn there was mist in his eyes. "You look like little ladies," he said.

"You sure do, sugar dumplin'." Logan swung Polly up into his lap. "You haven't seen the present your uncles got for you. You ready?"

"Yes, Uncle Logan."

"All right, Bryce," he called. "Bring it in."

Bryce opened the door and stomped in, carrying a load covered with a blanket. Polly jumped up and down. "What is it? What is it?"

"You have to open it, dumplin'. That's the rule at Christmas."

He set it down in front of her. Alisa gathered her breath at the lovely pint-sized saddle.

Polly's face grew serious, and she glanced at Logan and Bryce. "This is a nice saddle. Thank you very much."

The boys laughed along with the rest of the adults in the room. Ginny Mae had become fascinated with the dollhouse their uncle Paul had crafted.

Daniel grabbed his daughter's coat. "Let's go see what your

daddy got you for Christmas, sweetheart."

Alisa knew the girl was getting a pony. But as the rest of the family trekked outside to witness the child's joy, she hung back, needing a few moments of solitude. She began picking up the papers and spreading them out to be put away and reused. The box from Titus was burning a hole in her apron. She reached for it but pulled her hand away as though she'd touched a hot stove. No. She couldn't accept a gift from him and then leave. It sent the wrong message.

Oh, God. If only there was a way I could remain at the ranch with Titus.

What if she were to go back and proclaim her innocence? Even if the authorities didn't believe her, would it be better to run for the rest of her life or sit in jail? Possibly get hung for murder? She shuddered.

"You cold?" This time Titus's hands on her shoulders and the sound of his voice didn't startle her.

She shook her head. "Just thinking an unpleasant thought."

"On Christmas morning?" He turned her to face him. "That's not right. You're supposed to save unpleasant thoughts for the day after."

She smiled in spite of herself.

"You haven't opened my gift yet?"

"No." She pulled it from her pocket and offered him the box. "I can't accept this."

His face clouded with hurt. "But you don't even know what it is yet."

"It doesn't matter." She placed it in his hand and curled his fingers around the cardboard edges. "It isn't proper for me to accept a gift when I'm leaving in a few months. It's not fair to you."

He scowled and tossed the box onto the table. Then he took her by the shoulders and captured her gaze. "I want to know why you think you have to leave. I don't care what you have done in the past. I don't care who you're running from. I love you, and I'm not letting you go." His frown deepened. "You're not already married are you?"

"Of course not!"

"All right. Then tell me what's wrong!"

"Oh, Titus. . ." Suddenly, it all came tumbling out as it had weeks earlier with Mrs. White. Anger flared in his eyes as she ended her story with boarding the stagecoach.

"I'm so sorry, Alisa. I can't even imagine what it must have been like for you to finally find your father only to discover he's lower than a slug's belly. I'd like to—"

"Oh, please, Titus. God has given me the grace to forgive him. I even pray that God will give him a new heart. But now do you see why I can't stay here? Especially now that you know the truth. You are keeping a wanted woman from justice."

"It wouldn't be justice to send you back. As far as I'm concerned, you're not going anywhere. We'll get married the next time Parson Abe rides through."

She allowed herself to relax against his broad chest, wishing for all the world that she could accept his proposal and live her days building a life with this wonderful man of her dreams.

Apparently taking her silence as a yes, Titus relaxed as well. His large hand cupped her head. When she pulled back, he commanded her gaze with eyes filled with love and passion. Suddenly, he crushed her to him, his mouth covering hers. Slowly he softened the kiss, but his warm lips continued pressing against hers until she became breathless. The sensations flashing through her surprised and delighted her. . .and broke her heart. Unless she could clear her name, he would never be hers. She pressed closer and allowed herself another heady moment of being in his arms.

He pulled away as voices from the others came closer.

"I love you," he whispered.

Her lips trembled. "Titus Chance, I love you, too."

Tears clogged her throat. There was no choice now. She had to leave him before she lost the power to do so. With difficulty, she maintained a normal demeanor throughout the rest of the day.

That night after everyone had gone to bed and she was reasonably sure they slept, she rose and dressed with trembling fingers. Then she grabbed her coat and reticule and wrote a note for Titus, promising the return of his horse. Quietly, she left the cabin amid Daniel and Titus's snoring and made her way to the barn. Ten minutes later, she knew she'd made the biggest mistake of her life as two riders blocked the path in front of her.

"Amos, it looks like this is our lucky night."

"It sure it, Bart. It surely is."

≈

Titus jerked awake. Something didn't feel right. The fire had gone out, but that wasn't it. He stood and walked around the room. Glanced outside. Everything seemed quiet enough. Stepped back inside.

"What's wrong?" Gideon's sleepy voice asked.

"Not sure." He lit the lamp on the table and knocked on the post next to the bedroom. "Miriam, Alisa?"

"What are you doing, Titus?" Gideon was on his feet. "Miriam needs her sleep. Don't go waking her up on a hunch."

She appeared, clutching her robe about her, her face white. "Alisa's not here."

A lump lodged in Titus's throat. "We've got to go after her. If those two hurt her, I'll—"

"Titus, she left a note. She wasn't kidnapped."

He looked down at the paper she pushed into his hand.

"It's for you."

"Let's get you back to bed," Gideon said to his wife, but Titus knew they were giving him the chance to read the letter from Alisa in privacy.

His heart sank as he read the words:

Titus,

These last few months have been the happiest of my life. God used you as a sort of knight in shining armor to rescue me and bring me to the ranch. I don't know what I would have done without you. And I thank you from the bottom of my heart. Falling in love was the last thing on my mind, but I don't suppose we have a choice where our hearts are concerned. For I do love you, my Titus. I hope to return to you soon, but if I am not back within a year, I beg of you to forget me.

Yours,
Alisa

Forget her? How could she even suggest that was possible? No matter how many years went by, he'd never forget her. Didn't she understand that? Panic swelled his chest. Where could she have gone? He pulled on his boots and grabbed his hat.

She'd gone to turn herself in. And if she was right, her worthless father would see that she hung.

Oh, Lord. Help me find her.

He saddled Logan's horse, a stallion and the fastest of the horses on Chance Ranch since Raven had been stolen. Titus rode hard, the rising sun at his back. He only prayed she wasn't too far ahead for him to catch her before she turned herself in.

fifteen

"You men could have saved yourself the trouble. I was going back to turn myself in anyway."

Alisa knew she should probably keep her mouth shut, but she couldn't help goading the two bumbling thieves.

"Maybe so, sister, but I know a man who's willin' to pay five hundred dollars to see you handed over." Bart snarled. "And that's what we're gonna do."

Five-hundred dollars? It could only be Robert Worthington. But why was Robert, rather than the law, offering a reward for her?

"How did you two find out about me?"

Amos reached into his filthy coat pocket and produced an equally filthy paper. He pushed it toward her. She scowled and lifted her bound wrists for his perusal. "My hands are tied; you'll have to open it for me."

"Oh, yeah," he muttered. He unfolded the greasy paper.

Alisa's eyes went wide at the sight of her image staring back. "This isn't an official wanted poster, though?"

"Nope." Amos refolded the paper and replaced it in his coat pocket. "How come you're thinking the law's after you? You steal this feller's money or something? Looked like he has a lot of it."

"That's none of your business." She averted her gaze to let him know she was through speaking with him.

"Spunky little thang, ain't ya?"

139

"Not really."

"Can't we just keep her, Bart? I really like this one. She ain't so pretty as the one with all the curls, but at least she don't scream and cry like that one did."

Stung at the negative comparison to Prissy's painted beauty, Alisa felt the heat rise to her cheeks. She resisted the temptation to defend herself and concentrated on staying atop the horse despite her bound wrists—which were beginning to chafe along with other parts of her anatomy. She had never ridden before coming to the ranch and had only had a couple of lessons as it was. That she'd managed to avoid falling headlong to the muddy ground was a miracle indeed.

"You heard what Worthington said. No one touches her."

Robert hadn't wanted her harmed? Surprise and gratitude combined inside of Alisa to form a tender spot in her heart for her father.

"Yeah, but he wants her back pretty bad if you ask me. I'd bet my half of that reward that he'd take her however he can get her."

From his place in front of the two of them, Bart turned in his saddle and glared at Amos. "Keep yer hands off her or I'm gonna put a bullet through yer heart. I ain't takin' a chance on losing five hundred dollars because of somethin' you can get at just about any saloon in San Francisco."

Heat flared in Alisa's cheeks as she listened to the two argue, knowing there was nothing she could do about her predicament at the moment and praying fervently that Bart kept the upper hand on the other man.

Droplets of water splashed from the sky and hit her hands and her head. Soon the sprinkles became a soaking rain. A miserable rain that wouldn't let up. With muddy conditions being added to the already soft road, the ground soon became difficult for the horses to trudge through, and the going became nearly impossible.

Finally, Bart muttered a loud oath. "We're gonna have to hole up somewhere."

The thought of being "holed up" anywhere with these two immoral men made Alisa sick to her stomach. "I need my hands untied if I'm going to handle this horse without falling off," she said.

Her words were met with silence as the two concentrated on keeping their own horses upright.

"Bart!" Her voice shot through the steady stream falling from the sky. "I can't ride in this with my hands tied."

"Untie her so she'll shut up."

The other man made no move to obey.

Frustration and a real fear she was about to fall emboldened Alisa. "Bart!"

"Amos!"

"I can't. My horse ain't doin' so well."

"Fine," the brute growled. "Take my place at the front of the line. I'll untie her."

He maneuvered the animal around and rode back to Alisa's position. Amos moved carefully ahead, fighting for control. Alisa stopped her horse and held out her bound wrists.

Bart's dark gaze focused on her with an intensity that made her want to shrink back. Pure evil lurked beneath the surface of that gaze, and she silently prayed for protection. This man might be keeping Amos in line, but when he stared at her and roughly took hold of her clasped hands, she had trouble thanking the Lord for him. He brandished a ten-inch blade and sliced through the ropes. Alisa gasped as the knife's edge nicked her. Blood trickled down her hand toward her fingers. She winced at the pain. With a scowl he made a grab for her skirt.

"What are you doing?" she demanded, outrage suddenly eclipsing fear or pain.

He sliced a patch of the muslin and handed it to her. "Wrap this around that cut. And don't flatter yerself. Ain't no woman alive worth five hundred dollars—not to me anyways. I'm warning you," he snarled. "If you take off, I'll come after you and let Amos test that theory that Worthington'll take you however he can get you back. Understand?"

Unable to speak for the terrifying image conjured up by his words, Alisa nodded and grabbed onto the reins.

After another tense hour of concentrating on keeping the horses from slipping and falling, the trio spotted a farmhouse in the distance.

"We'll hole up in the barn," Bart announced.

"We can't just ride up to a person's barn. Someone's gonna see us."

"If you don't act stupid, no one'll suspect we're anything more than three travelers needin' a dry place to rest. I'm gonna knock on the door and ask."

Relief swept over Alisa at the thought of getting out of the rain. But along with the relief came the worrisome thought of spending any time alone with these two. On the other hand, if the people who lived in the farmhouse knew she was there, perhaps she could somehow convey her predicament and find a rescuer.

As if reading her thoughts, Bart curled his lip. "Don't make me slice your throat."

She swallowed hard and nodded. Only God could get her

out of the situation. As long as Bart was in charge, she felt reasonably safe.

The next seconds seemed as a dream. As Bart urged his horse forward, the animal lost its footing in the mire. The burly outlaw's arms flailed as he went down. He landed with a thud, and the mount landed atop him, then quickly righted itself. But Bart remained where he'd fallen. Alisa dismounted quickly and slogged through the mud until she reached him. Her stomach roiled at the sight of his leg, twisted under him in an unnatural position. One didn't need to be a physician to recognize the severity of his broken leg.

"You gettin' up, Bart?" Amos called. "Yer the one who said we need to get goin'."

"He's badly hurt. He won't make it without our help."

Amos cursed and dismounted. He stomped back to where Bart lay. His face drained of color. "This is bad, Bart."

"You ain't sayin' nothin' I don't already know," Bart grunted, then clenched his teeth.

Alisa stared at Amos, waiting for him to instruct her as to how they would get his partner the next couple of hundred yards to the farmhouse. Confusion spread over his face.

"We'll have to help him," she prompted.

Amos scowled. "I know that!"

Obviously threatened by her instruction, the man turned his attention once more to Bart, who was beginning to lose consciousness. Alarm filled Alisa. She knew it would be difficult enough to move Bart with his help, but his dead weight in these conditions would be next to impossible.

"Bart," she said, kneeling beside him, "try to stay with us. We're going to need your help supporting part of your weight while we move you. Do you understand what I'm saying?"

Without opening his eyes, he nodded. "I'm tryin'."

Compassion rose inside of Alisa. "I know you are," she soothed. "I'm going to try to straighten your leg." She glanced at Amos. "Is there anything he can bite down on to help control the pain?"

"Ya mean like chewin' tobacco?"

Alisa sighed. This idiot would be no help. "No. I mean something hard that he can't bite in two. Like a heavy branch or something."

Amos slogged to the nearest tree and luckily had the presence of mind to hack off a branch thick enough for their purposes. He whittled away the leaves. "Will this do?"

Nodding, Alisa took the heavy stick. "Open your mouth, Bart. I want you to clamp down on this while we straighten your leg."

Fear lit his eyes, but he nodded and did as she instructed.

"Will you help me?" she asked Amos.

"He's gonna kill me if I hurt 'im."

"He'll be grateful you cared enough to help him."

Amos sneered. "Don't think this nursin' business is gonna make us let you go. 'Cuz it ain't."

"That's the last thing on my mind. Let's get Bart out of this mud for now."

A scream of agony tore from Bart, and the stick fell to the ground as he passed out. Despair filled Alisa. How on earth would they get him to the barn now?

"We're going to have to go for help."

"No we ain't, girlie." Amos grabbed onto her arm and yanked her to her feet. "Leave 'im. He's more than likely gonna be dead by mornin' anyways."

A gasped escaped her throat. "We can't leave him. What if

it were you? Would you want us to leave you?"

He gave a short, bitter laugh. "Mark my words. If I was dumb enough to fall off my horse, Bart'd leave me without lookin' back."

Alisa had to admit to herself that he probably had a point. Still, she had to try to make him see reason. "Amos, Jesus said we are to do unto others as we would have them do unto us. If you were hurt, you'd want Bart to help you."

He frowned as though the words were too much for him.

Help me, Jesus.

"If you had fallen off your horse, I would be interceding for you just as I am now for Bart. Please reconsider."

"Stop yer yammerin'."

Alisa's shoulders slumped in defeat, until none-too-gently Amos hefted Bart up and slung him over his shoulder. She nearly gasped in surprise at the strength he demonstrated. She followed as he muscled Bart over the horse, who seemed not to be injured from the ordeal.

"Thank you, Amos. You did the right thing."

He grunted. "Probably the dumbest thing I ever done. Get back on your horse, and let's get goin'."

Fingers of fear crawled up her spine as his gaze slid over her. A slow smile lifted his mouth.

What was she going to do when her only protection was injured and unconscious?

&

Titus spoke gently to the horse, urging it forward. "I know you want out of this rain, and I don't blame you. Fact is, so do I. But Alisa needs me, and I'm going to find her. And you're my partner." It hadn't taken long on the trail for him to realize that though Alisa had started out alone, two other riders had quickly joined her. He felt nearly strangled by the thought of who those two men most likely were. They were ruthless men, and he prayed for strength not to act out of vengeance if they hurt Alisa.

He knew the danger of plodding on in this mud and rain, especially now that night had fallen. All day he'd seen signs of the three horses trying to stay afoot. But he knew the outlaws would have to hole up eventually. And that was when he planned to make his move.

Father, lead me to her.

❧

Alisa smiled and handed the middle-aged woman a tray containing the swept-clean plates. The gracious couple who owned the farm had helped set Bart's leg and had offered Amos and Alisa a place in the house for the night. Amos had declined, stating the foolish lie that he and Alisa were on their honeymoon and preferred to be alone in the barn. Mortified, Alisa tried to be impassive, but she was almost certain the woman's eyes flickered with concern. If only there was some way to clarify her position as a hostage without taking a chance that Amos might harm the couple.

After lighting the lantern, the woman, whose slightly graying hair was pinned neatly into a bun at the nape of her neck, smiled. "Well, I brung you some extra blankets. I set 'em over there in the corner. Wish I could offer you some dry clothes, but my only other dress is wet, too."

Alisa smiled. "I appreciate all you've done. You've been very kind."

The woman flushed. "Ain't no more'n anyone else woulda done. Yer welcome to stay 'til it's safe to travel in this mud." She glanced at Amos. "If you'd like to follow me to the house,

I can spare a fresh shirt of my husband's."

A grin stretched Amos's mouth. "Don't mind if I do."

Resisting the urge to beg her to stay, Alisa watched the woman slip through the barn door with Amos on her heels.

Bart moaned from his bed of hay at the end of the barn. Amos refused to allow even Bart to stay in the house. "I'm in charge now," he boasted. "Bart ain't gettin' no soft bed if I ain't."

Alisa hadn't reminded him that he'd had his chance for a real bed and turned it down. She didn't want to encourage his memory as to the real reason he was sleeping in the barn.

She lifted a blanket from the stack and spread it over Bart's shivering body. If they could have built a fire, she would have insisted he get out of the wet clothes, but again, no sense giving Amos any ideas.

She sat back against the wall and watched Bart's white face and trembling body. He needed a doctor. Had the horse landing on him injured more than just his leg? He'd begun to awaken by the time their hosts had begun the task of setting the leg and the woman had offered laudanum, which Alisa had encouraged. Now Bart slept and didn't have to endure the pain.

It was almost certain that Amos would leave him behind. She prayed the five hundred dollar reward would be enough to discourage Amos from keeping her captive. She stood on legs wobbly from the day's ride. Why hadn't she snuck out when Amos left? Hurrying toward the door, she paused only a minute to grab an extra blanket. Heart in her throat, she reached the door and flung it open. She stepped into the night. She gasped as Amos's stubbly face loomed in front of her like something from a nightmare.

"Get back inside," he ordered.

Silently, she obeyed, tentacles of fear clutching her belly.

"You know what I want, girlie. And Bart ain't in no position to keep me from it."

"Amos, please," she croaked, backing up. "Don't do this."

"Save yer breath," he snarled. In a flash, he grabbed her arm and pulled her roughly to him. Alisa fought wildly, flailing hands and feet. She screamed. Amos clamped his hand over her mouth. She twisted and shook her head until his hand slipped enough for her to bite down.

"Yeow!" His hand came up in a terrifying moment.

She saw the sheer hatred in his eyes just before his hand slammed into her face and pain exploded in the side of her head.

sixteen

Titus heard the gut-wrenching cry tear from his throat as though it came from outside his body. The sight of that filthy, foul man touching Alisa, manhandling her, attempting to violate her was more than his very soul could take. Everything in him wanted to draw his pistol and shoot, but he couldn't take a chance on harming Alisa.

He rushed forward and clamped down on Amos's coat with both hands and, with strength he didn't know he possessed, flung him away from Alisa and onto the ground. Titus grabbed his gun from his holster and pointed it toward Amos, using all of his control to refrain from squeezing the trigger and sending a bullet into the man's skull.

A stream of profanity flew from the outlaw's mouth, fouling the air as much as his stench.

"Get out of the way, Alisa," Titus ordered and, from the corner of his eye, noted that she backed toward the other side of the barn.

Amos quickly regained his footing and started to go for his gun.

"I wouldn't," Titus warned. "Real slow-like. Take the gun out and toss it this way."

Keeping his hate-filled eyes fixed on Titus, Amos reached for his gun and eased it out of the holster. "I shoulda killed you the night I took this Colt off of you."

"Probably," Titus replied, matching him sneer for sneer.

"Bart, no!"

At Alisa's scream, Titus's world slowed its spinning. Just as Titus turned to the woman he loved, he saw Amos lunge from the corner of his eye.

❧

Horror filled Alisa, and she made a dash for Bart. She kicked at his arm as hard as she could. Gunfire filled the barn as his pistol flew from his hand. He hollered and reached for her, but she jumped back in time to avoid his massive hand.

The sound of Titus's grunt brought her about, a sense of dread knifing into her gut. He lay on the ground, Amos stretched sideways across him.

She rushed to his side. He pushed at Amos's lifeless body. "Help me get him off of me," Titus said.

She helped him roll Amos aside. "You killed him, Titus. I'm so sorry." Her heart nearly broke for him at the necessity of taking a man's life.

He took her into his arms and held her tight, as though clinging to life. "I didn't," he whispered against her hair. "I would shoot him to protect you. But I didn't fire my gun. I didn't have time."

Frowning, Alisa pulled away. "What do you mean?" Then she turned to Bart as realization dawned. "You shot your partner?"

Bart grimaced. "I'd rather take my chances in jail than be at the mercy of that snake."

"I. . .I thought you were trying to shoot Titus."

He responded with silence, his eyes closed.

Alisa turned in Titus's arms. "Are you all right?"

"I am now. Did they hurt you?"

Heat rose to her cheeks. "No."

"Praise the Lord."

The barn door opened, and Mr. Meyers stood, rifle in hand, ready to defend his home. "What's going on in here?"

Titus quickly explained the situation. Mrs. Meyers slipped her arm around Alisa's shoulders. "I could just kick myself for not following my instincts. I knew a sweet, young thing like you wouldn't take up with the likes of those vermin."

"It's all right," Alisa assured her. "But if you don't mind, I will accept the hospitality of your extra bed."

"Of course." She bustled Alisa inside while the men tended to Amos's body.

They spent the next four days waiting for the rain to stop and the ground to firm up enough for safe travel. Alisa avoided time alone with Titus as much as possible. She knew by his possessiveness that he considered their future sealed. But the fact still remained that she had to turn herself in and hope for God's justice to prevail. Otherwise she would never have a life with Titus. But she didn't bother to tell him. She knew it wouldn't do any good.

On the morning of the fifth day, he found her on the front porch enjoying a glorious pink and blue sunrise. He slipped his arm about her waist and pulled her against his side. A sigh escaped her as she gave herself to the moment and rested her head on his shoulder.

"This is just the first of many sunrises we'll share," he said, his voice wrought with emotion and longing.

Oh, how she wished that were true. And it could be, but only if God willed. First she had to take care of anything that might cause them or their children harm.

Titus shifted, and Alisa raised her head from his shoulder. He turned her to face him, his hands warm on her arms.

"Alisa," he said, capturing her gaze with blue pools filled with love. "I want to talk to you about something. . .ask you. . ."

Her heart lurched, and she quickly pressed a finger to his lips. "Now isn't the time."

Disappointment evident in his features, he dropped his hands and nodded. "I suppose you're right."

"Are you going for the sheriff or taking Bart in?"

"I've been working on a travois to carry him. That way he can lie down, and the horse can drag him along behind. I don't want to burden the Meyers with him until the law picks him up."

"It's probably for the best."

"I plan to leave this morning. But I've already spoken to Mr. and Mrs. Meyers, and they'd be pleased to have you stay on until I come back. I'm leaving Logan's horse as well as Raven here. San Francisco is only a few hours away. It'll take me a little longer, having to go slow so as not to cause Bart any more pain—not that he doesn't deserve it."

"You're considerate," she said softly. "God must love that about you."

Tenderness softened his features. He reached out and trailed a line from her cheekbone to her jaw. "There's so many things God must love about you, I can't even begin to name them all." He stepped closer, and Alisa had neither the strength nor the desire to protest as he pulled her to him. He pressed his forehead to hers. "There are so many things I love about you, too," he whispered. "So many things."

She took in the wonder of his gaze sweeping over her face as though he were memorizing every contour. His mouth settled on hers, and before she could summon a thought, Alisa felt his lips on hers, warm and so very soft. His tenderness brought tears to Alisa's eyes. How she loved this man. She allowed herself the sweetness of his embrace, and in that moment, for the first time in her life, she felt cherished.

Titus pulled away, and concern filled his eyes. "You're crying."

She nodded, unable to speak for the emotion clogging her throat. He pulled her into his embrace once more. Cupping her head, he pressed it against his shoulder. She was so relieved that he didn't demand an explanation for the tears. Didn't condemn himself unnecessarily for kissing her. It was as though he understood her feelings, understood she was overwhelmed with all the events of the past months that had led to this moment—the moment she understood once and for all that she was precious and worthy of the love of a good man. And of the love of God as He'd displayed time and again, watching over her with loving care, guiding her to the people who would be His hands to her.

She wrapped her arms around Titus's waist and snuggled into his warmth. They remained locked in a tender embrace until the smells of frying bacon and brewing coffee wafted onto the porch, serving as a reminder that the world didn't belong to only them.

❧

Titus blinked at the sheriff, fearing for a moment he hadn't fully understood the wonderful words coming from the man's gravelly throat. After delivering the outlaws, one dead, one alive, to the sheriff, Titus had been compelled to ask about Alisa. Now, faced with the answer, he couldn't believe what he was hearing. "You mean Alisa Worthington isn't wanted for murder?"

"Already told you. The old lady weren't murdered. Doc says her heart gave out. She hit her head on the way down."

"Then why would Alisa have thought she was wanted?"

The sheriff gave a heavy sigh and leaned his chair back on two legs. He laced his fingers over an ample gut and frowned in concentration. "If memory serves, it had something to do with the old lady's son accusing the girl. Seems she was holding onto Miz Worthington when the lady died. The whole thing was a mite confusing if you ask me."

"How so?"

"Seems the girl was raised an orphan. . ." The sheriff launched into the tale, his story matching the one Alisa had shared with him. But then he continued. "Miz Worthington left her big, fancy house and all her money—loads of it—to the girl. That son of hers gets most of the shipping company, which will bring him enough to be one of the richest men in town, but he wants it all. I guess that's why he offered the reward for the girl."

Trying to assimilate the information that Alisa was now a wealthy young woman, Titus pressed his fists to the desk and leaned forward. "Do you think he intends her harm to get his hands on her inheritance?"

The sheriff dismissed the concern with the shake of his head. "Naw. He's not dumb enough to do that. I figure he's going to try to talk her out of it."

Fury ignited Titus at the thought of this man trying to weasel Alisa's inheritance from her.

"Where can I find this Robert Worthington?"

The sheriff eyed him. "I don't want no trouble."

"Neither do I. But it just so happens that I'm in love with his daughter and plan on marrying her as soon as I get back home. I just want to see that he cancels the reward for her return. I don't want to be constantly looking over my shoulder afraid some lowlife like Bart is going to try to take my wife away."

The sheriff nodded. He gave him directions to the street. "Can't miss it. It's the big brick house—covers most of the block."

❧

Alisa guided Raven down the familiar streets of San Francisco. She'd waited until the morning after Titus left before borrowing Raven and heading west toward the city. He'd know where she was going, but by the time he got back to the Meyers' and back to San Francisco, it would be too late for him to stop her from turning herself in. She had had time to reflect while she rode the few hours alone. A curious sense of peace enveloped her, a reassurance inside that all was well. That God would forever remain on His throne in her heart regardless of the struggles she might have to endure.

She refused to allow herself to think of the possibility that she might go free, refused to hope for the best. Time had taught her that. Time and one disappointment after another. Mr. and Mrs. Perryman had been kind guardians, but they never pretended they were mother and father. They had a calling to place children with good Christian parents. Their love was evident, but even so, they couldn't shield any of their young charges from the cruelty of other children or the pain of being rejected by possible parents. Over and over again— more times than Alisa could, or cared to, remember. But all in all, Alisa had been happy, especially during her later years at the orphanage when she finally understood that she wouldn't be adopted and she might as well throw herself into making life a little sweeter for the younger children.

Alisa pulled Raven to a stop in front of the orphanage. Before she did anything else, she needed to see her little family.

To tell Mrs. Perryman all about Titus. To tell them all good-bye just in case she was locked up for a long, long time. The front gate groaned as she opened it and groaned again when she shut it behind her. Her heart nearly broke at the sight of the sagging porch, the house that had been her home in such need of repair and painting. She knocked and waited. And waited. Then tried the knob. Locked? The orphanage doors were never locked. Not even at night. Worry flashed through her. Had the orphanage been closed down? Where were Mrs. Perryman and the children?

"You looking to adopt?"

Alisa turned to find Miss Smithers, the woman who occupied the home next door.

"No. I'm—"

"Why, Alisa! I recognize you."

"Hello, Miss Smithers." She walked down the steps and met the elderly woman at the gate. "Where are Mrs. Perryman and the children?"

"Gone. The roof at the back of the house finally caved in."

"Oh, my." She hadn't noticed the roof from her view.

"It was a blessing in disguise if you ask me. Those children are better off now."

"What do you mean?" Alisa asked, gently touching the woman's arm to bring her back to focus.

"Don't you know?" She smiled broadly. "They're staying at the Worthington house. Can you imagine those orphans running around that big place?"

seventeen

Alisa rode Raven as fast as she could all the way across town until she reached the Worthington home. She stared at the massive brick structure and shuddered at the memories it conjured. Tears stung her eyes as she realized that Mrs. Worthington's beautiful smile wouldn't greet her when she entered the ornate foyer. Or ever again.

She climbed the steps, her heart beating wildly in her ears. Grabbing the brass knocker, she hesitated. An image of Mr. Worthington's face, red with fury, passed through her mind. Would he order her from the house? Her hands trembled as she slowly lifted the ring and brought it down, lifted it again and knocked once more.

Marietta, Mrs. Worthington's longtime housekeeper, opened the door. Her face split into a smile. "Alisa! You've come home." Stepping aside, she allowed Alisa to enter the familiar home, the home her grandmother had left to her, though Alisa knew it would never be hers.

"How have you been, Marietta?" she asked, catching the woman into a quick embrace.

"Lonely." The simple word brought tears to Alisa's eyes. She reached for the older woman's hand.

"I know what you mean. This house seems much bigger without her, doesn't it?"

Before she could answer, a crash sounded from the parlor just beyond the foyer.

"Look what you did," a child's voice cried. "We're going to get thrown out of here now."

Marietta huffed. "I'm much too old to run after children."

Alisa followed her toward the parlor. "Why are they here?"

"Young Robert has taken a liking to them, I suppose." She scowled and opened the parlor door. A vase—one that looked expensive—lay in pieces on the floor. Sarah and Sammy Baker, six-year-old twins who had come to the orphanage two years earlier after both parents succumbed to influenza, trembled before Marietta. "We're sorry," Sarah whispered. "It was an accident."

Sammy's gaze darted away from Marietta's stern face, and his brown eyes widened, then a smile pushed his chubby cheeks out even farther. "Alisa! You've come back. We live here now."

Alisa returned his tight hug. "I'm so glad to see you."

What did he mean, they lived here now? She turned her questioning gaze on Marietta. The housekeeper clapped her hands together and gave the children a stern frown. "Run along and find the broom and clean up this mess. It's a mighty good thing for you the ugly vase was already cracked." Alisa hid her smile as the contrite children slid by. Sammy looked back at her before heading out of the room. "You still going to be here when we get back?"

She nodded. "I'll be here."

When the children had gone, Marietta shook her head. "Those two get into more trouble. . . ."

"How long have they been living here, Marietta?"

"Since Christmas Day."

"Christmas?"

She knelt and began picking up the big pieces of the vase.

"Mr. Worthington was invited to the orphanage for Christmas dinner, seeing as how he donated a sizable amount of money for the children's Christmas."

"He did?"

She sat back on her heels. "Wouldn't have thought it of him, would you?"

Too stunned to speak, Alisa shook her head.

"Anyway, while they were enjoying a Christmas goose—"

"A goose?" Oh, God was so good. Every year since she was a child, Alisa remembered Mrs. Perryman's lament over the lack of a Christmas goose.

"Goose. Anyway, the way the children tell it, they were just finishing up their dinner when all of a sudden the roof gave way under the weight of all that rainwater. It flooded the kitchen and ruined the pies."

"And Mr. Worthington brought them here?" It was a little hard not to question his motives, given their last encounter.

"That's right. Packed up the lot of them and tucked them into bed upstairs."

The place certainly was large enough. She could imagine the thrill the children must be feeling to have gone from a dilapidated old home to this mansion. When she'd come to be Mrs. Worthington's companion, Alisa had felt like she was living in a palace. She frowned. But just like in her situation, this arrangement wouldn't last. The children would be on the streets if Mrs. Perryman couldn't fix the roof. And how could she? She could barely feed the children, which was why the house was in such desperate need of repair in the first place.

"Alisa!"

Alisa turned toward the door at the sound of Mrs. Perryman's voice. She rushed toward the only mother she'd ever known and ran into her arms. Mrs. Perryman's voice shook with tears. "It's true. You really are here."

"Yes. But I don't understand all of this. Marietta explained why you're here. But how. . ."

"I invited them, of course."

Alisa gasped and took an instinctive step back as Mr. Worthington strode into the room. "And I hope they'll stay as long as necessary."

Mrs. Perryman fingered her collar and averted her gaze to the Turkish rug on the floor. Her cheeks grew pink as Mr. Worthington came to stand beside her. Alisa's eyes widened then narrowed in suspicion. "What are you playing at, sir?" she asked, indignation beginning to build within her.

"I'm not playing at anything. I'm merely offering this good woman and the children in her care a home since theirs is unlivable." He frowned. "I would have thought this would make you happy."

"It would. . .I mean it does." Alisa looked from her father to Mrs. Perryman. "May I speak to you in private, Mr. Worthington?"

"Of course." He turned to Mrs. Perryman. "Please excuse us for a few moments. My daughter and I have some things to discuss."

Alisa's throat tightened, and she felt suspiciously close to tears at his words. If only this scoundrel really meant what he said. She followed in silence as he led her to his office. "Please have a seat," he offered, motioning toward a pair of brown leather chairs.

"Thank you," she replied stiffly. To her surprise, he took the other chair rather than walking around the desk and sitting as she'd seem him do many times with guests and business associates.

"You're all right?" he asked. Was that guilt hiding in his eyes?

She sniffed. "If by your inquiry you mean did Bart and Amos harm me, no they did not—no thanks to you."

That was most definitely relief washing across his face. What was he playing at?

"I understand Amos is dead and Bart has been placed in jail?"

Alisa frowned. "That's right. How did you know that?"

"Your young man came to see me yesterday."

"My young. . .Titus was here?"

"Yes, and he seems to be under the impression that you're safely tucked away at a farmhouse between here and his ranch." He peered at her closely. "Why have you come back?"

"To turn myself in."

His eyes widened, and he sucked in a sharp breath. "For something you didn't do?"

"I hope to plead my case to the authorities. Perhaps the judge will be lenient."

Moisture formed in his eyes, and his shoulders slumped as he leaned forward and reached for her hands.

Alisa shrank back.

"Don't be frightened," he said.

At the soft, almost defeated tone, Alisa allowed him to take her hands in both of his. "What's come over you, Mr. Worthington? I don't understand."

"I know. Bear with me for a few minutes, and I'll explain."

Alisa nodded, praying that God would give her wisdom to know the truth.

"When Mother announced she was giving you the house and the money already accrued from the shipping company, I was furious. Shocked. Betrayed."

"But Mr. Worthington, I never—"

He nodded. "I know. You didn't even know that you're my daughter."

Hearing him say the words sent a jolt through her. She stared at him and for the first time saw the truth. This man was her father; his blood flowed through her veins. They had the same nose that turned up slightly at the end, the same brown eyes, and the same creases in their cheeks that hinted at dimples when they smiled. Which he did at that moment.

"It's a little overwhelming when it comes to you, isn't it?"

"Yes, sir," she whispered.

"Over the past few months, my life without my mother has been lonely, and I realized that I would gladly give up everything, including the shipping company, to have her back." He gave a short laugh. "She would love to hear that. Mother always believed I had great potential, but I never believed I could make it without the allowance she bestowed upon me each month.

"But as lonely as I've been, I started thinking what it must have been like to grow up without either a mother or a father."

"I had Mrs. Perryman."

His expression softened. "I have high regard for Mrs. Perryman. She's a rare jewel indeed."

A rare jewel? Alisa peered closer. Was her father falling in love with Mrs. Perryman? She captured her bottom lip between her teeth in order to stave off a smile.

He smiled, obviously reading her amusement. "As I said, she's a remarkable woman."

"What about Bart and Amos?"

"They came to me after reading the poster. At the time, I still hadn't come to grips with everything, and against my better judgment, I gave them the okay to find you."

"You instructed them not to harm me."

"You're my daughter. I couldn't bear the thought."

"Why were you looking for me?"

He heaved a sigh. "At first, of course, I wanted you to sign away your rights to the house and money."

"I never wanted—"

Again he silenced her. "I know you didn't ask for anything. But mother loved you. I wish the two of you could have established a familial relationship. Even so, she had grown to know you over the months you worked for us while she was making arrangements for your future. It was her desire to give you the house and the money. And in doing so, she did me a great favor."

"A favor?"

"I'm learning the shipping company. Even gave Jonesy a job there in the office running errands and learning the books."

"What a wonderful position for Jonesy! He's so good with numbers."

Her father nodded, and Alisa felt warm all over. "I discovered that pretty early on. He has a head for sales, too. I expect he'll move up and be a successful man himself some day."

The pride reflected in her father's face piqued her curiosity. He answered her question before she asked. "I'd like to know how you would feel if I were to adopt Jonesy. Give him my name—our name—and ask him to join me in the business."

"Oh, Mr. Worthington." Tears burned her throat and eyes. "Have you spoken with Jonesy yet?"

"No. First I wanted to see how you felt."

"But why?"

"I've denied you—my flesh and blood—the right to a father for twenty years. I would spend the rest of my life making it up to you if you want me to. Devoting all of my attention on you and any grandchildren you give me."

"You mean you want to be sure I don't mind sharing you?" Alisa laughed.

He reddened. "I understand. It was a ludicrous thing to even suggest you might want a relationship with me. Forgive my presumption."

"No, that's not it. I'm amazed by all of this. Really."

"So am I, to be honest. Now, to get down to business matters. I assume you will live on your husband's ranch?"

"Oh, well. Titus and I do need to speak of matters now that things have changed." And she wasn't going to jail. Joy welled up inside her and curved her lips into a smile. There was nothing keeping them apart now. It was all she could do not to jump back on Raven and fly all the way home to the man she loved.

"Will you be selling the house?"

"Sell Titus's house? There are several cabins all together. It wouldn't be right to sell one of them to a stranger. Besides, Titus would never leave his family."

His mouth twisted to one side in a smile. "I meant this house," he drawled.

"How could I? I mean, why would I sell your house?"

"Alisa," he said, keeping his gaze steady on her. "It's your house. Mother left it to you."

"Oh." Was it really true? She hadn't been dreaming it all this time? Even in her wildest imagination, it never occurred to her that anyone would actually let her have it.

"Do you want it?" she asked her father. Something flickered in his eyes.

"I am preparing to buy my own home. The company brings in much more than I realized, and I am financially secure."

"But wouldn't you rather stay in the home where you grew up?"

"I must admit I would. But the house is large. Much too large for a man alone."

Alisa smiled as understanding dawned. "You've offered Mrs. Perryman and the children a place to stay for as long as they need."

"Yes."

"Would you object if I turn the house over to them for good?"

He expelled a breath and smiled as though relieved. "I had hoped you would consider that an option."

"D. . .do I have enough money to maintain the house for them?"

He chuckled. "My dear, you have enough money to maintain a hundred houses for them. You are an extremely wealthy young lady. Not to mention the fact that twenty-five percent of the shipping company belongs to you as well."

Alisa's eyes widened. "Oh." If she hadn't already been sitting, she would certainly have felt the need to do so. She remembered the conversation between Robert and Mrs. Worthington before the horrendous scene that followed. All the inheritance talk had been eclipsed by the appalling aftermath.

"You're remembering." He said the words as a statement, not a question. "I'm so sorry."

"Mr. Worthington, I forgive you for accusing me. I know your mother had sprung the news on you as suddenly as I heard it myself."

"I want to know you, Alisa. You're so much like your grandmother." He squeezed her hands. "I know I don't deserve the opportunity to know you. But I've changed, and I pray God will give me the chance to prove it."

"I. . .I would like the chance to know you, too." It was too hard to say *Father* just yet. She wasn't ready. But some day, she hoped their relationship would be such that her children would have the benefit of a real grandfather.

"Where is she?" A roar from the foyer interrupted them. Robert shot to his feet, releasing Alisa's hands. The door burst open, and Titus strode through.

Alisa gasped. "Titus!"

"Why did you leave?" he demanded. "I thought I told you'd I'd be coming back."

"If you'll excuse me," Robert said, coughing into his fist. "I'll leave you two alone to talk things over."

"Well?"

Alisa frowned. "If you'll calm down, I can explain."

His breathing slowed a bit, and he looked into her eyes, tenderness replacing the hard edges of only a second ago. Alisa smiled. This was the Titus she knew.

"I was worried sick about you riding alone to San Francisco. When Mrs. Meyers told me you'd ridden here, I thought you had come to turn yourself in."

"There's no reason for me to."

"I know. I talked it over with the sheriff yesterday."

"Robert said you came to see him as well."

Titus nodded. He stepped forward and gathered her

around the waist, pulling her close. Alisa didn't resist. On the contrary, she willingly stepped into his embrace and wrapped her arms around his neck.

"Why did you come to see Robert?"

He brushed her upturned lips with his. "I wanted to be sure no one else was going to be coming after my wife."

Alisa grinned. "Have you a wife, Titus Chance?"

"I will have before the day's out, if you're willing to marry me before we go home."

"So soon? Won't your family be upset?"

"We can throw a barbeque for all the neighbors to celebrate. But if we wait, there's no telling when Parson Abe's coming back. If weather keeps him from his appointed time next month, it could be another three months." He dipped his head and brushed her lips again. "I don't want to wait that long to marry you." His husky voice sent a shiver down Alisa's spine, and she found herself nodding in agreement when he said, "Let's go find a preacher."

"Perhaps we could find one to come here? I'd love to have Mrs. Perryman and the children in attendance."

"And your father?"

She nodded. "Yes. Him, too. And Titus, before I become your wife, I would like to ask a favor."

"Anything, my love."

"I want to sign this house over to Mrs. Perryman."

"The house?"

"My grandmother left it for me."

His eyes grew soft and thoughtful. "I think it's a wonderful idea to leave it to the children."

"There's more. I. . .I, well, we'll never have to worry about money, Titus."

"I've never been worried about it." He grinned and kissed her. "But I have the feeling you have more news."

"According to Mr. Worthington, I'm apparently quite wealthy. Please say I can share it with you."

"My brothers are pretty determined to make the ranch a success on their own. But I'm sure if we get in a bind, they'd agree to take a little help. At any rate, the money will be there for our children."

"Yes, our children."

His gaze captured hers, revealing all the love she could ever have imagined possible. When he lowered his head and pressed his lips to hers, his arms tightened about her. Locked in his embrace, Alisa returned his kiss, knowing that God had truly taken the horror of the past few months and turned them into something good.

epilogue

Alisa's eyes misted with tears as she and Titus waved good-bye to the group at the doorway. Her father and Mrs. Perryman and all of the children, including Jonesy, were on hand to wish them well.

Titus grabbed the reins then hesitated. "We could stay one more day if you want."

Alisa smiled at her new husband and leaned her head against his shoulder. They had been married for a little over a week, staying at one of San Francisco's finest hotels during most of that time. She'd met with Mr. Chadwick, the lawyer handling her grandmother's estate, and had settled everything so that Mrs. Perryman would never have to worry again. Best of all, with the new home, they could accommodate up to ten more children. Alisa had loved every moment of her time with them all, and a seed had been planted for a loving relationship with her father, but she was eager to begin her life as Mrs. Titus Chance in their own home. She squeezed his arm. "No. It's time to go home."

"I agree," he said, taking his attention off the road for a moment to kiss her soundly. "It was generous of your father to insist you take a few things of your grandmother's."

Alisa twisted in the seat and eyed the pile of furniture she was taking back. Two beds, one for her and Titus to share and one for Miriam and Gideon—a belated wedding present. Poor Miriam's back was beginning to hurt her from the uncomfortable straw mattress she'd had to endure. Then there was the pie safe she'd fallen in love with from the moment she entered the kitchen, and the Turkish rug from the library. Some chairs. She loved the idea of being able to contribute to the home somehow.

"Did you mention the furniture we're bringing back when you telegraphed the family?"

Titus grinned. "Nope. Just told them I was bringing home my bride and to move my things back into the cabin."

Alisa's cheeks warmed, but she snuggled closer to her husband. "Good. Then it will be like Christmas all over again."

"That reminds me." Titus stopped the wagon and reached into his pocket, producing the box he'd given her at Christmas. "Merry Christmas."

"Oh, Titus." She opened the box, and a soft gasp escaped at the sight of the lovely cameo pin inside. "It's beautiful. I love it."

Despite the fact that they were stopped on a crowded street, Titus pulled her close. "You're beautiful, and I love you." He lowered his face to hers and kissed her. As they resumed their journey, Alisa's heart sang with thankfulness to God. Though she'd been raised an orphan, He hadn't left her fatherless forever. He'd sent her to a large, loving family and, more important, to a man who would love and cherish her for the rest of her life. She knew that she'd never be alone again.

A Letter To Our Readers

Dear Reader:

In order that we might better contribute to your reading enjoyment, we would appreciate your taking a few minutes to respond to the following questions. We welcome your comments and read each form and letter we receive. When completed, please return to the following:

Fiction Editor
Heartsong Presents
PO Box 719
Uhrichsville, Ohio 44683

1. Did you enjoy reading *Second Chance* by Tracey V. Bateman?
   ❏ Very much! I would like to see more books by this author!
   ❏ Moderately. I would have enjoyed it more if

   _____

   _____

   _____

2. Are you a member of **Heartsong Presents**? ❏ Yes ❏ No
   If no, where did you purchase this book? _____

   _____

3. How would you rate, on a scale from 1 (poor) to 5 (superior), the cover design? _____

4. On a scale from 1 (poor) to 10 (superior), please rate the following elements.

   _____ Heroine   _____ Plot
   _____ Hero   _____ Inspirational theme
   _____ Setting   _____ Secondary characters

5. These characters were special because?_____
_____
_____

6. How has this book inspired your life?_____
_____
_____

7. What settings would you like to see covered in future
   Heartsong Presents books? _____
_____
_____

8. What are some inspirational themes you would like to see
   treated in future books? _____
_____
_____

9. Would you be interested in reading other **Heartsong
   Presents** titles? ❏ Yes ❏ No

10. Please check your age range:
    ❏ Under 18   ❏ 18-24
    ❏ 25-34   ❏ 35-45
    ❏ 46-55   ❏ Over 55

Name_____
Occupation _____
Address _____
City_____ State_____ Zip_____

COLORADO

4 stories in 1

Taming the frontier is a daunting task—one that can't be burdened by the luxuries of life, including romance. Four settlers take the challenge and are surprised when love springs up beside them along the way.

Four complete inspirational romance stories by author Rosey Dow.

Historical, paperback, 464 pages, 5 ³/₁₆" x 8"

❤ ❤ ❤ ❤ ❤ ❤ ❤ ❤ ❤ ❤ ❤ ❤ ❤ ❤ ❤ ❤

❤ ❤ ❤ ❤ ❤ ❤ ❤ ❤ ❤ ❤ ❤ ❤ ❤ ❤ ❤ ❤

$\mathcal{H}$EARTSONG ❤ PRESENTS
Love Stories Are Rated G!

That's for godly, gratifying, and of course, great! If you love a thrilling love story but don't appreciate the sordidness of some popular paperback romances, **Heartsong Presents** is for you. In fact, **Heartsong Presents** is the premiere inspirational romance book club featuring love stories where Christian faith is the primary ingredient in a marriage relationship.

Sign up today to receive your first set of four, never-before-published Christian romances. Send no money now; you will receive a bill with the first shipment. You may cancel at any time without obligation, and if you aren't completely satisfied with any selection, you may return the books for an immediate refund!

Imagine. . .four new romances every four weeks—two historical, two contemporary—with men and women like you who long to meet the one God has chosen as the love of their lives. . .all for the low price of $10.99 postpaid.

To join, simply complete the coupon below and mail to the address provided. **Heartsong Presents** romances are rated G for another reason: They'll arrive Godspeed!